WLA Folios: Peace

Copyright © 2017 War, Literature & the Arts
All rights reserved.
ISBN: 1546372784
ISBN-13: 978-1546372783

The views expressed in this publication are those of the authors and do not necessarily reflect the official policy or position of the United States Air Force Academy, the Air Force, the Department of Defense, or the U.S. Government

TABLE OF CONTENTS

JESSE GOOLSBY

EDITOR, *WLA FOLIOS*

For nearly 30 years *War, Literature & the Arts: An International Journal of the Humanities* has published work that illuminates the vital confluence of conflict and art. We're proud of our history of showcasing established and emerging voices across a wide spectrum of genres. Our new venture, *WLA Folios,* is an important contribution to *WLA*'s present and future.

Published every year in the spring, *WLA Folios* is a themed issue which complements and magnifies the annual journal while staking out new ground. For 2017, the focus of *WLA Folios* is peace. Sixteen distinguished contributors were asked to consider peace and its many manifestations, voices, reflections, corruptions, memories, and aspirations. I'm honored to share the results with you here.

ROXANA ROBINSON

Peace

What do we mean by "Peace?"

Maybe the word conjures up the image of a broad landscape, tall grasses, shady trees, a distant horizon. Animals or humans somewhere, grazing or working quietly. My own vision would contain living beings. Outer space would be absent of strife, but it would be empty. For me, peace requires living presence.

But just to be alive means struggle. We're in a state of constant struggle just within our own bodies, lungs going in and out, hearts thudding, brains and nerves doing their mysterious work. We're fighting off bacteria and infections, creating new cells. We struggle for survival through competition with other living organisms: we rip carrots from the ground, catch fish from the sea, cause animals to be slaughtered. We struggle in other ways: we disagree with others. We argue with our neighbors and our family. We try to make the world different.

We create conflict. We've all felt warlike impulses. We feel a rushing surge of anger, the will to supersede, compete, challenge, obliterate. To attack. Maybe to kill. The impulse is visceral and emotional rather than cerebral. It's driven by adrenaline and some mad interior logic: *Just do it!*

These feelings have consequences. If we do attack someone, afterwards, when the adrenaline drains away, it leaves us feeling isolated. We've separated ourselves from the community we've attacked. We've drawn a line between us and them. But these warlike impulses are human, we all feel them to some degree.

We've all felt peaceful impulses, too. We know the wish to forgive, understand, embrace. Cherish and protect and empathise. These are also driven by something visceral and interior, not by the rational brain. And they have consequences, too. After we act on those impulses we feel connected to the community, to the rest of humanity.

Neither is permanent. The state of war can't be sustained indefinitely; the human soul wears out. And after a time of peace the horror of war fades in the collective memory, and warlike urges recur, often from a new generation.

Peace must exist in the midst of these opposing forces. It's not the absence of conflict, but an active, constructive response.

My favorite image of peace comes from a book I read, years ago, about an African tribe of bushmen called the !Kung. (As I remember it, the "!" represents a click sound). The !Kung lived in the Kalahari Desert, and during the 1950s a pair of American anthropologists lived with them and studied them. They became very close to the tribe. (I should acknowledge that today this arrangement seems condescending and colonialist. I'm not condoning it.) The book was written by their daughter.

The !Kung were small in stature, but great in skill and effectiveness. They were impressive for many reasons, but one was that they were essentially nonviolent. When a member of the tribe broke their rules, they shunned him until he recanted. They made him leave the tribe, and in the Kalahari Desert, isolation meant death. The only way to survive was through cooperation, sharing energy and resources. So it was interesting that in such a wild and challenging landscape, their own survival strategy was a peaceful one.

But the best part of the story was not about the way the tribe got along with their members, but about the way they got along with their rivals.

The Kalahari Desert was a harsh landscape, mostly arid and nearly barren. Survival there took place within narrow margins. The inhabitants had highly evolved survival strategies.

The !Kung were omnivores, which meant they were carnivores. This put them into direct competition with another apex predator: Panthera leo, the great African lion.

In the natural world, creatures have survival strategies. A cougar will target the smallest and weakest deer in a herd. Not because of cowardice but practicality: he can't risk attack by a big powerful animal who could gore him or break a rib with his kick. A wounded animal can die quickly, from infection, or slowly, from starvation, if he's too weak to hunt. So a predator chooses animals weaker than he.

Predators who share the same territory and hunt the same prey are competitors, and so exist in a constant state of tension.

The bushmen and the lions had shared the same territory for hundreds of years, maybe thousands. They hunted the same prey – grazing animals, gazelles, giraffes and their friends. But they left each other alone.

Instead, they had a system. The !Kung were bowhunters, and when they shot a giraffe they might wound but not kill him. The long-legged animal would set off through the brush, moving faster than the hunters, who followed by tracking his bloody trail. It might take several days for the giraffe to die. When he finally came down, collapsing into a huge heap among the desert foliage, the hunters might be hours away. The carcass would wait for the scavengers. Sometimes the first of these to arrive, drawn by the smell, was a lion. Sometimes more than one lion.

I remember the description of one these encounters. The giraffe's huge corpse is on the desert floor. Two lions, male and female, lie stretched out beside it, faces pressed against the body. They're gnawing on the flesh. The lions hear the bushmen coming through the bush, and the male turns slightly, watching, but he keeps eating. The bushmen come closer and the lions begin to growl. When the hunters appear in the clearing the lions flatten their ears and begin to growl. They go on eating, snapping and gulping, but their eyes follow the bushmen. The hunters walk upright, carrying their bows at their sides. They greet the lions and begin to talk, walking up and down in the clearing. They tell the lions that they are eating a giraffe that belongs to the !Kung. We shot him, they say, You know that. We tracked him for three days, and now he is dead. He is ours. You must leave him alone.

The bushmen walk back and forth, dignified, respectful, insistent. They are not angry. They shake their heads and wag their fingers at the lion, talking in clear, certain tones. The lions growl, lashing their tails back and forth, watching from the corners of their eyes. They bite the carcass, bolting mouthfuls of meat. No, say the bushman, you must stop. It is our giraffe. They come closer, walking slowly and confidently, sure of their moral rights. They shake their heads, admonishing the lions. The male lion, his great tail thumping the earth, his ears flat with displeasure, his lips drawn back, tears into the giraffe's flesh. But he's listening. Finally he raises his head, tossing his dark mane and snarling. The hunters do not stop. They wag their fingers at him, shaking their heads. It is ours, they said. You know that. Leave him.

First the male, then the female, crawl backward, snarling, moving away from the giraffe. Then they spring to their feet, crouching low. They watch the hunters, growling, as they slide toward the edge of the clearing. There they turn; they vanish into the brush. The hunters wait for a moment, out of courtesy and also out of prudence, then they settle in to cut up the carcass. They know the lions are there in the bush, watching. When the hunters have finished cutting up the meat they leave something for the lions.

Essential to this outcome is respect: for each other, and for the rule of law. The hunters didn't interfere with the lion's prey when he brought it down himself, which meant they had the moral authority to demand that he leave them their prey when they had brought it down. They both obeyed a rule of law. For thousands of years, lions and !Kung, both apex predators, survived in a state of peaceful coexistence.

The reason I raise this is that I think peace is an active state, not a passive one. It's not merely the absence of dispute, it's an active commitment to a non-violent resolution.

Humans aren't limited now to finger-wagging admonitions, in order to persuade others of our ideas. We have more tools of every sort. We have better methods of communication, more ways of predicting responses and understanding them.

And we have more powerful weapons: now we could kill that giraffe within seconds of seeing it, as well as any lion that approached it. Would that double kill mean the cessation of conflict? Would that be peace? Is that what peace means, a state in which everyone is frightened of the one who carries the biggest weapon?

What kind of peace would that be? How would we feel if we were the ones who didn't have the biggest weapon? If we were the ones moving quietly from tree to tree, staying in the shadows and hoping that the person with the rifle doesn't see us, or doesn't dislike us, or doesn't see us as a threat? Would that feel like peace?

What is it that creates peace? Can peace be one-sided, or would that be conquest? Does an occupied country feel at peace? Who is in charge of peace? What does peace have to do with power?

It seems to me that real peace, like the peace between the !Kung and their leonine neighbors, is one which power and responsibility are shared, and in which all the members of the community are respected. There is no peace without rule of law; without it you will never know when your peace will be violated. The lions knew that the !Kung would not steal their prey; the !Kung knew that the lions would not ambush them when they left. The !Kung and the lions were not friends, but they were members of the same community and they obeyed the same laws. They respected each other. Through respect they established trust, and trust is what makes peace possible.

These things don't occur in a vacuum, they require constant action. Peace is not a passive state. We must respect our neighbors and we must obey our laws. We must contribute to a state of trust. It's trust that produces the politics of peace across the globe. Peace requires more than simply feeling empathy and brotherhood, it requires a means of resolving conflict. We are human; we will disagree. We must find a resolution. Peace requires commitment, engagement, struggle. Struggle, of course, is how we live, so we may as well struggle toward peace.

Think of those hunters, walking up and down, stating the law, and the lions listening. Everyone paying attention.

No war. Peace.

ROXANA ROBINSON is the author of five novels, including *Cost*; three collections of short stories; and the biography *Georgia O'Keeffe: A Life*. Her work has appeared in *The New Yorker, The Atlantic, Harper's Magazine, The New York Times, The Washington Post, The Wall Street Journal, Bookforum*, and *Tin House,* among other publications. Her latest novel, *Sparta*, received the James Webb Award for Distinguished Fiction from the USMC Heritage Foundation. She was recently elected president of the Authors Guild.

NATHALIE HANDAL

Une Fin

There will be no broken chair, no unlit lamp, no left conversation, there will be no crushed galaxies, we will memorize the Greek gods for clarity and pray to the Roman gods for liberty, Aragon will guide us, we will no longer turn blue of wound in the empty rooms of after lives, we will no longer be bruised, our bodies folded in half like forgotten fairytales, like the beaten frame of doors where we declared our name. What's a land, what's a land? The country we pretend to go to when we can't find the form of our faces. We will never see the sea the way we saw it together nor the wind that push us back into an old language we refuse to forget, like a book unopened after decades, the pages braced together. Where are the gods in our blames? But let's not leave yet. After all, we've just arrived.

NATHALIE HANDAL was raised in Latin America, France and the Arab world, and educated in the United States and United Kingdom. Poet, playwright and literary travel writer, her recent books include the flash collection *The Republics*, winner of the Virginia Faulkner Award for Excellence in Writing and Arab American Book Award; the bestselling bilingual collection *La estrella invisible / The Invisible Star*; the critically acclaimed *Poet in Andalucía*; and *Love and Strange Horses*, winner of the Gold Medal Independent Publisher Book Award. Handal is a Lannan Foundation Fellow,

Centro Andaluz de las Letras Fellow, Fondazione di Venezia Fellow, and winner of the Alejo Zuloaga Order in Literature, among other honors. She is a professor at Columbia University and writes the column The City and the Writer for Words without Borders.

JULIAN ZABALBEASCOA

Catalunya

They were waiting in a forest, the old man tells me, the first ones. Over the ridge there. He points at the sloping mountain line to our right that tapers into the sea.

They were still in Spain? I ask, and he nods.

I was, and he trails off. Twelve? Every paper showed a parade. Tanks in the street. Women sitting on soldiers' laps, their right arms outstretched in a salute. Finally, my father kept saying, finally that mess is over. What had been the trouble, I wondered. It looked like more fun than we were having but then you saw the buildings, those that still stood.

He stops and drinks his whiskey. Together we look past the scattered pines before us onto the beach, a wide belt of sand, wider than any I've seen. From the patio, the water is a small stripe along the horizon. The rest is beach.

It makes sense, no, why they brought them here? he asks. When he learned of it, my father cursed to whoever would listen as though it mattered. He made every threat he could. But those in Paris didn't care. The *gendarmes* hammered in posts to keep us from our beach and stretched a mesh of hooks across it. Then the people emerged. You see those trees over there? I follow his finger to a thick, zigzagging line of dark green that follows a fold in the mountains. That was nothing compared to the column of people spilling out of their side of Catalunya. It didn't seem a country could have held them all, let alone a forest. It was impossible this beach would. Yet here they came, and for weeks they didn't stop.

The *gendarmes* enthusiastically tapped those first ones with batons but they were defeated creatures. I stood on the sidewalk with my dad and some of his friends. Women held children's hands while balancing suitcases bound with twine on their heads. A woman with a crutch, one pant leg knotted at the knee, even managed it. The men were loaded down like mares. They walked bow-headed toward the beach. Then I saw something of a curious sight approach. A boy my age pulled along an emaciated sheep. You'd have thought the war had burnt every last herb in Spain. The boy and his sheep were the only two that met our eyes. I wondered about the journey they'd made together when a man near us on the sidewalk stepped into the street and grabbed the rope from the boy. The boy resisted, there was a brief struggle, but then he received a hard knock from a *gendarme* and the sheep went with the man. I expected my dad to say something. He squinted at the smoke he exhaled.

How long will they be here? I asked, but nobody answered.

The boy lunged for his sheep. This time the *gendarme* lifted the baton over his head. I flinched for the sound it made. *Allez!* he yelled and kicked at the boy. Onward! The boy was holding a side of his face. An older man – I don't know how many tattered blankets were tied around him – helped the boy off the ground, with the *gendarme* behind them continuing to yell – *Allez! Allez!* – and wave his baton.

Early on, one of those first evenings, some friends and I couldn't resist this great curiosity. Gran Hotel du Catalunya, we were calling it. The wind came off the water at a cruel angle, as sharp as the barbwire perimeter. *Gendarmes* patrolled with little interest. Mostly they huddled together, their collars up, passing a bottle between them under hastily constructed sentry boxes whose roofs and floors were little more than sieves. Lorries were scattered at the edge of the coastline. Those *gendarmes* pulling higher rank sat in them, occasionally wiping the condensation from the windows to glance at the beach. The wind rattled the chains in the truck beds. The rain blurred our vision as we crawled closer to the fence.

He stops. This place has changed, he says. Back then there wasn't any of this. He waves at the apartment buildings down the street, the shops and restaurants, even, it seems, the asphalt. I can't position myself in it as easily. Who knows, he says, it may have been this very spot where my friends and I approached the fence. Look at those *sauvages*, my friend laughed. We got the language from our fathers, of course. But watching them on the beach, it made sense. Their desperation was vulgar. It disgusted us, and we pointed and giggled while we watched them dig at the sand like a bitch about to give birth. In the days to come they'd collect enough driftwood to construct tents but that night our giggles turned to uncontrollable laughter for their frantic burrowing.

I was up early the next morning with my father. He cursed at those inside when he saw the grey bodies tumbling in the surf. They ultimately pulled their own from the water and buried them in the least desired spot on the beach, but the tide would uproot them like Lazarus and at dawn, once more, they'd roll loose-limbed in the waves.

He scratches at the side of his face. That was the world once, he says as though drawing a curtain on his story.

Once?

Who knows. He signals for the server and points at his empty glass. You, too? he asks. I finish mine and nod. *Hé*, he calls at the server. She's my age, a year or two out of college. The old man points at both our glasses, and she nods then goes inside.

So what is it exactly you're trying to find? the old man asks after she brings our drinks.

A story.

Whose story?

I shrug.

You say your grandfather was here? He lifts his chin at the beach.

Yes, but not till later.

How much later?

Toward the end. He was probably one of the last few to cross.

Describe him for me.

The swell rises, distinct from the others, as it builds toward the shore. We watch it spread, overtake another, then tilt and curl until it breaks. The old man is nodding. White floaters cordon off an area for swimming though the red triangle flag cautions anyone from entering the water. A few banners for French companies catch the wind and tug on the poles they're tied to.

We had befriended a few *gendarmes*, he says, my friends and I. They'd take us in their lorries, and we'd drive along the border with them. On my own, at that age, I wouldn't have dared it. He points to the mountain range. I had nightmares about what was on the Spanish side of Catalunya. Over there was so bad that people wouldn't trade all of the hunger and sorrow of the beach for it. I feared getting too close lest it somehow pull me in. But with the sun above me and at the *gendarmes'* side, I felt invincible.

One of my friends spotted them—a handful of Spanish soldiers. We were in the lorry's bed, and he shouted and banged on the truck's roof, pointing. The truck bounced over the road to them. I'd never seen a sadder lot. Our *gendarmes* were clean-shaven, wore crisp uniforms, at the right angle their buttons caught the light. But these soldiers were hollow-cheeked, sooty, each a collection of bones dragging itself forward. Exhausted, they didn't acknowledge us as we approached. The lorry pulled alongside them, and one of the *gendarmes* muttered a few words of what probably passed for Spanish. He yanked his thumb in the direction of our town and the beach. The soldiers' lips were thin, that's what I noticed. They were cracked, split wide at every crease, burned of any moisture. Their eyes were set deep into their skulls. They had paused for a moment as the *gendarme* spoke to them but then resumed their pace as though we weren't there.

A *gendarme* swore at them. Another yelled, We don't have all day. He called our names and we jumped from the bed and they drove around the soldiers to come behind them. The *gendarme* on the passenger side slapped the outside of the door and hollered. The truck's grill nearly clipped their backsides. We were alongside them shouting – *Allez!* *Allez!* – like collies pushing a flock of sheep. They started jogging and soon we were on the road. *Allez!* Onward! He shakes his head. I remember that, all the way to town, to the beach and its human smell and everything else that awaited them there, the gravel under my feet – *Allez! Allez!* – smiling as I ran.

––––––––––

JULIAN ZABALBEASCOA lives in Boston and is a visiting professor in the Honors College at University of Massachusetts of Lowell. "Catalunya" is the eighth in a collection of linked stories. The first seven have appeared in *American Short Fiction*, *Gettysburg Review*, *Glimmer Train*, *Ploughshares*, *Post Road*, *Shenandoah*, and *Southern Indiana Review*.

M A R I L Y N   K A L L E T

Falling Out

According to *Le Monde*, *désamour* reigns
between nations, which means
falling out of love,

Triptik
to forget it.
Dice your love

and make
a tapenade.
Serve on hard toast.

I have tried falling out,
my yearning
more rock wall

than slide.
Let's scale
down,

de-escalate
to mere
crush.

Désamour.
Désamour mucho.
Can't come back

to never.
What does wind
know, stripping limbs?

According to *Le Monde,*
there has been a
decrescendo,

but in my dreams
your face is sharp,
foreground to infinity.

You are
mountains
waving yoo-hoo

to molehills,
nothing gained or lost.
In this country of mistrals

you are no less
beautiful,
at home in fierce wind.

I translate your flesh
into words,
your beauty

a touch
less ravaging
in song.

MARILYN KALLET was born in Montgomery, Alabama, and grew up in New York. She is the author of 17 books, including recently a translation of Parisian poet Chantal Bizzini's *Disenchanted City*, co-edited with J. Bradford Anderson and co-translated with Anderson and D. Jackson, and *The Love That Moves Me*, poetry from Black Widow Press; *Packing Light: New and Selected Poems*, Black Widow Press; *Circe, After Hours*, poetry from BkMk Press; *The Big Game*, translation of Surrealist poet Benjamin Péret, 2011, and *Last Love Poems of Paul Eluard*, both from Black Widow Press. Kallet is Nancy Moore Goslee Professor of English at the University of Tennessee in Knoxville.

S T E V E N   K I S T U L E N T Z

The Closest We Have Ever Come

One afternoon, in the middle of that Cosby era of nothingness known as the 1980's, my father made his final devotion to the television. All his adult life, television had been his most intimate friend, from the Kennedy assassination to man on the moon, to the ABC movie of the week, to reruns of *Hogan's Heroes*. He chose what the family watched; my only job was to learn what I could about the mostly silent man as he stared at his favorite shows, the simple morality plays in black and white that retold the most mainstream version of World War II. We watched them all, the classic movies, John Wayne squinting and shouting his way through *The Longest Day*, the preposterous arrogance of *A Bridge Too Far*, George C. Scott in his parade gloss boots and mirror-finish helmet, even mediocrities like *Force 10 from Navarone*.

After he retired, he spent what would be his final months wasting away in a brown velvet Barcalounger, alternately distracted and enthralled by his newly installed cable. He'd been devoted to television for some time, watching the various iterations of World War II, especially the episodic retellings of *Combat!* The men of *Combat!* the series fought their way across the same parts of the French countryside where my father had been dropped in 1944. He often quoted a line from the first episode, Vic Morrow's Sgt. Saunders justifying the off-camera killing of a German infantry man by saying, "A tank looks down your throat, you do what you think is best. There was nothing else to do."

Whenever the events covered an infantry unit in France or Germany in the eleven months between D-Day and V-E Day, Dad would supplement the film with a short narration about his own service. They say that when you know you are about to die, your life flashes in front of your eyes, but I know now that when the dying becomes months long and tedious, you watch it on television.

The only other thing he watched was the news.

The background narration to our family dinners was provided by Marvin Kalb in Saigon, Bert Quint at the Pentagon, Daniel Schorr in Washington, Eric Sevareid with a comment, the stentorian announcements of the *CBS Evening News with Walter Cronkite.* We weren't allowed to talk, not my mother, not my sister who'd sewed a "War is not healthy for people and other living things" patch on her denim jacket. The rule was silence as we watched Dan Rather in an M-65 jacket, reporting alongside the men of the 1ˢᵗ Marines. It had always been this way, through Nixon's final days and through Whip Inflation Now and through, "My name is Jimmy Carter and I want to be your President." And in his final months, my father became obsessed with the minutiae of a shadowy deal where an American colonel sold Israeli anti-tank weapons to the Iranian government, then funneled the proceeds to anti-communist rebels in Nicaragua.

In that short a summary, the Iran-Contra affair reads like a preposterous, unpublishable spy novel. A 26-year-old aide took a chartered plane carrying millions in cash and travelers checks to El Salvador, handed the money over to a Contra rebel, and returned to DC in time to get hammered in Dewey Beach that weekend. A secretary with a high school diploma shredded some of the nation's secrets, carried others to her car stuffed into her panties, an offense for which full-bird Colonels have gone to prison. And so for a week, her panties were the subject of national news, having been apparently purchased by a Marine Corps Lieutenant Colonel, her boss.

Pictures of the Colonel were themselves national news. He stood upright, right hand raised, taking the oath before he testified before a select committee of the United States Congress. The committee was tasked with investigating the illegal sales of arms by the U.S. government to anti-communist rebels fighting a vague and ineffective insurrection against the Sandinistas, the Marxist-inspired government that ruled Nicaragua.

The committee was chaired by Daniel Inouye, Democrat of Hawaii. He rarely invoked his status as a war hero, and truthfully, he did not need to, as he was missing an arm from the war; the empty sleeve stood as a potent reminder of his service, his sacrifice. In front of the television, I learned Senator Inouye was a law school classmate of my father's, a surprising bit of information, since I hadn't known that my father had gone to law school.

There was a lot I hadn't known. Information had always been, in this household, on a need-to-know basis. And frequently, in the eyes of my father, I had no need to know.

I came home from my sophomore year of college in the first week of May 1987. The hearings had just begun, but Dad was already embedded on the couch, gripped by the pressing question of the day, *What did the President know and when did he know it?* It felt surreal and familiar, the same questions from the Watergate hearings a decade and a half before, as the Select Committee chaired by Sam Ervin broadcast gavel-to-gavel coverage of Nixon's self-destruction.

Dad had been gripped by those hearings too; the House Subcommittee on Criminal Justice was chaired then by an old infantry buddy, Bill Hungate of Missouri, and Dad took the seven-year-old me to watch a day of the hearings from the anterooms of the House Judiciary Committee. During a lunch recess, I sat in Chairman Peter Rodino's chair and banged the chairman's gavel, hitting the oak striking block so firmly that the print reporters covering the day all rushed into the room, to find that the sole person on the dais was.

My father was a man who had been a lifelong conservative, who ran for the school board in Lucerne County, Pennsylvania in 1956 as a Republican, in an era when Pennsylvania politics were machine operations dominated by the United Mine Workers. His brother Mike, a UMW member, faced a tough choice: vote for a Republican, or vote against his brother; he chose neither, instead running away to nearby Hazleton and its larger VFW bar, and by that simple choice, demonstrated that maybe Uncle Mike was the best politician in the family. Now, during each recess of the Iran-Contra hearings, Dad would turn to me and ask about the proceedings. Did I see what was happening here? Did I understand how *we*, that royal *we* that meant every American citizen, had lost our basic sense of moral clarity? With each passing afternoon, he grew increasingly distraught.

It wasn't until July, during the testimony of Admiral John Poindexter, President Reagan's National Security Advisor, that my father began to prosecute the case he'd been building in his head all summer. "You do understand what this is," he'd say, assuming I did but not waiting for an answer. "This is senior military officials directly contravening the law of the land."

I shrugged. I hadn't given it much, if any, thought. My friends plastered their cars with bumper stickers that offered pithy, of-the-moment endorsements of Lieutenant Colonel Oliver North, Admiral Poindexter, General Richard Secord, all the unindicted co-conspirators of this latest scandal. One said, *Nicaragua is Spanish for Afghanistan.* When Colonel North raised his right hand to testify, a number of my classmates went out and got regulation haircuts, a modified high and tight that declared their fealty to the ideas of duty and country they saw celebrated in the Colonel's class A uniform, its impressive array of career fruit salad.

"What this is," Dad said on his way to retrieve a beer from the refrigerator, "is the closest we have ever come to a military coup in this country."

I didn't hear that sort of alarm anywhere else. This was all about freedom fighters, someone on the radio told me. I was commuting, 45 minutes a day, from a job as a gopher at one the Washington's oldest and largest law firms, where the elderly, bespoke-suited men I passed in the halls were the same elderly and bespoke-suited men I saw on the Sunday morning talk shows, talking about the Colonel and his arms for hostages schemes.

It was a great summer job, replete with free dinners and paid parking and a $13 an hour paycheck, which meant that overtime was the kind of golden money that irresponsible 20-year-olds dream about. The clients were a who's who of famous miscreants, Ivan Boesky, Ted Bundy. I was just politically astute enough to notice that Boesky's criminal defense wouldn't pay paralegals any overtime, but Ted Bundy's death penalty appeal had seemingly endless pockets, even though the firm was handling it pro bono.

Was it the closest we'd ever come to a coup? Unlikely. I know now, at a remove of nearly thirty years, that what my father struggled for all his life was a chance to return to the kind of sharpened moral clarity he knew as a 22-year-old infantry sergeant. His entire young life had been the simple narrative of good versus evil, unions versus management, the common man against the tyrant, democracy against communism, the hard-working good man against the crooked oligarch who ran the local building and loan, a world defined by the binary oppositions of a world where everything made sense. How little had made sense to him since the war? Years of hope, days of rage, a nation coming apart at the seams, towns poisoned by industry, a President who left office in disgrace, the unindicted coconspirator that he was. Only the war had made sense. He called it *the last just cause*.

If you think that is simple and overly reductive and makes for a sad story, that is your right and privilege; to me, it is an illustration of how television shapes what we learn, how we learn, and ultimately, who we love and how we love them.

In those shared moments, lit by the cathode glow of an ungainly Magnavox console, I learned all I ever would about my father. Which is woefully little. But I am grateful for the stories. How in the winter of 1944, he took a rabbit fur jacket off a dead German infantryman; how he deflated the tires of a headquarters company truck to pass under the only intact bridge on the Saar River later that spring. How he captured two German soldiers who were eavesdropping on Easter Sunday mass, April 1945, and how one of the Germans held a rosary in one hand and a .25 caliber Belgian Mauser pistol in the other. How I know now, at a distance of three intervening decades, that television for him was not just entertainment or distraction. It was a time machine, something that took him back to the only period in his life when things truly made sense, the days of physical training and close order drill and the unknowing bond of shared sacrifice, when the sides were clearly drawn, perhaps the last moments in his life where certain victory belonged to the righteous and just.

It gave him, in a word, peace.

STEVE KISTULENTZ is the Director of the Saint Leo Master of Arts in Creative Writing Program and an Associate Professor of English. He is the author of two collections of poetry, *Little Black Daydream* (2012), an editor's choice selection in the University of Akron Press Series in Poetry, and *The Luckless Age* (2010), selected from over 700 manuscripts as the winner of the Benjamin Saltman Award. His short stories have appeared in many journals, including *Narrative Magazine, Quarter After Eight, Crab Orchard Review*, and *Mississippi Review*. He earned a BA in English from the College of William and Mary, an MA from the Johns Hopkins University, an MFA from the Iowa Writer's Workshop, and a PhD from the Florida State University.

ODIE LINDSEY

Panoleah

Leah knew him so well that she could even read his wince. Though no more than a note on the accordion of his crow's feet, she could decipher any twitch as a marker of hurt or humor, surprise or fury. It could be a synaptic beat of confusion—or hell, just a simple tic.

In theory, her attunement could bring a new life somewhere else, administering to people crushed by stroke, and who communicated in glances and sighs.

Only, she would never get out of this house. She could never, ever leave him.

They sat on a couch in his neglected postwar prefab, on the throwaway side of Pitchlynn, Mississippi. The wall clock ticked in the pine-panel room. The air was a clot of rotted nylon carpet and wet summer air. The mannequin in the corner wore ACU camo and Interceptor body armor. Salvaged from the alley behind an athletic wear store in town, its head was now outfitted in a beige *shemagh* and polycarb ballistic shades.

Van Dorn had just asked Leah if she liked horses; she should have said *Yes*, or *No*, or better yet, *I don't know—you?* Instead, the question had flushed her memory of the man called New Father, a recollection so acute she had reeled off four sentences before catching Van Dorn's wince...and shutting up.

The silence was now pregnant with anxiety. She flinched when he cleared his throat.

"I hate horses," he said. "They's just too expensive for anybody not rich."

"Of course," she replied. "I'm over it now. Horses."

She couldn't help but smile. Because this was the beautiful thing about Van Dorn: he, too, had learned so much from their conditioning. Six months ago, her outburst would have provoked contusive instruction. Care of his fist, or his pliers, or whatever was around him—she would have experienced pain. Yet today, now, he had noted the speed and sincerity of her adjustment to the wince…and he had forgiven her just as quickly.

They were tranquil, at last. "Twinned," he called it.

* * *

Her mother was mostly Choctaw and some black. A storyteller, she had most often regaled young Leah about the ladybug—the "luckybug"—as a symbol, a gift to their family, and their world. "A trickster," her mother had claimed; if ants attacked the ladybug, for instance, the insect would fake its own death, emitting a terrible odor until left alone.

When Leah was five, an oven-hot autumn brought a plague of gnats into their trailer. Within days, the insects had lay dead on every surface, a holocaust of crust over every window sill and counter top, plate or piece of fruit.

The ladybugs followed, to feed on the gnats. Leah's mother, far from disgusted, had instead become ripe with laughter. She treated the swarm like the family's own personal windfall, and was ecstatic when counting the bugs' spots.

"Katsi'nonwí:io, girl!" her mother sang out, ladybugs trickling across her arms and neck. "Nine dots are lucky—and so, so rare. This is a gift from god, Panoleah. Like you."

Panoleah was Leah's full name, though nobody else had called her that. During the time when Van Dorn had still needed to curb her, when she still wore the collar, she would think of her mother and the ladybugs and spots, and of her full name, Panoleah. This memory had at first helped her get through the process; she cherished the strength it brought her. Ultimately, however, she realized that the letting go of individuation would prove pivotal to their development, and to the methodical elimination of conflict.

We are so nearly tuned, she thought now, grinning. It was exactly as Van Dorn had promised.

"You're hungry," she said.

"I am," he confirmed.

* * *

She'd been adopted once before. Her patron, Theodore Hollis, was the runoff from a north Mississippi heritage clan, a shunned trustee who lived on a former plantation outside of town. Hollis, who would ask Leah to call him New Father, had first been prone to visitation with her mom. For several months, he had shown up at their trailer on a regular basis, bearing trinkets: imported bottles and delicacies, or sometimes just hand-me-down, tall tales. Leah's mom called him "Old Man," though Theo was middle aged. He was generous and jokey, and he made everyone feel good; he could sit and sip at the kitchenette table for hours, wooing Leah's mother over a marathon of Spades (draw, no deal). Now and again he'd wink at Leah and ask if she wanted to play "52 Pickup," a gag she only fell for once.

Over the months, Hollis's affections had drifted to the child. Instead of marriage to Leah's mother, one night he had proposed a stewardship of the girl. He was kidding, of course—or so thought her mom. Soon enough, however, Hollis had cast out a line of sober promises about private schooling, new clothes, and a bedroom of her own. Princessdom.

Panoleah was 14, and the narrative bristled like magic. She had griped to her mother about wanting it, *needing* it. She moaned and had wept over how unfair it was not to have it, until eventually, Leah's mother had ordered her to go on, get. To figure out how the spider spun his web.

Of the many things that marked Leah's time with New Father, she mostly remembered his horses. A drove of failed Tennessee Walkers, geldings, they'd been rescued from an illegal breeder farm outside of Maryville. Their hooves had been sored in an attempt to manufacture gait, so they were slightly hobbled at a trot.

Leah spent every available instant with the animals, going so far as to sleep in a paddock. In reply, Hollis had bragged to her that he was the one who had saved them. Sheltered them. Fed them. Loved.

A few months into the arrangement, it became clear to Leah that New Father was also keeping her as a pet. She ran away soon after, home to her mother at first, and then on to whomever could comfort her.

* * *

Van Dorn first saw her at a moldering two-story motel, where he'd holed up to drink and remember the war, and accelerate the process of dying. The place was rented hourly or weekly. Migrant pickers clustered like vermin in the mildewed rooms. At evening, old men gathered plastic lawn chairs in the parking lot and lit trash fires.

A rotating squad of dropouts from the county high school threw parties at the motel—but always on the second floor. The boys brought in black girls and white girls, and whatever girls they could corral. The lot of them banged bass thump music and chuffed weed by the brick, and mixed prescription cough syrup with Mountain Dew and hard candy. Their huge American sedans were painted in carnival hues of purple and red, like the cars down in New Orleans, with LCD screens embedded in the back of the headrests, and trunks full of knockoff, kicker box speakers. They rode on 22-inch chrome rims like charioteers of the backwoods blacktops, in and out of the motel lot at all times of night, carting the girls around, hollering.

Van Dorn loved them. They were the realest, most vibrant people he could have ever fought for.

Some nights, though, late, he had to pull his boots on and stomp up the metal-cement stairway, and lay into them. Blocking their open doorway, shirtless, his dog tags flat against his slick, taut chest, his reaper tattoo, he would order them to shut it the fuck down. And he didn't care who he was talking to, and the kids were never too wasted to not take him seriously.

Except once, on the night he took her.

Early that evening, he'd been sitting in a lawn chair just outside his motel room, a tallboy in a bag in his hand. Leah and her girlfriend had walked up out of nowhere. She had long black hair, almond-y skin, was skinny. A tricky rap lyric tripped out of her lips as she passed him, glancing over. Seconds later, after she was out of sight, Van Dorn had heard her describe him as a "broke ass" to her friend. The girls had laughed.

He didn't care.

At least, he didn't want to. Still. As twilight leached away, the open doors of the party rooms above him burning yellow against the night; as the kids leaned against the second floor retaining grate, flicking their cigs into the parking lot, Van Dorn couldn't stop looking up, for her. At some point, he had even gone inside his room to watch television, to try and close himself off.

Every bass rattle had reminded him of a blast concussion. The crack of every beer can dropped on concrete was a rifle shot. The dancing had pummeled his ceiling for hours, until at some point he had stormed up the stairs.

One of the party boys pulled a weapon. Van Dorn marched straight into the pistol, its barrel denting his bare chest. When the boy, 17 or so, but with some pretty good muscles, began to unleash a torrent of threat, Van Dorn had snatched the gun away in a blur, snapping young man's carpal bones in the process. He then offered the pistol to anyone who would take up the challenge.

Nobody did.

Scanning the room for hostiles, he saw the girl sitting Indian style on the splotchy brown bedspread. She was the only one who had met his stare. He paused, then marched over and yanked her up by her arm. She giggled as he led her out, and down the stairs.

He sat her on his motel bed, and offered her a Coke. She refused, so he'd given her the remote control. They could hear the boys above hollering about what they would do to him.   The chorus of them sounded exactly like what they were: boys.

Van Dorn slept on the floor that night. Her first thought after he dozed was to go back upstairs and get high. She was seventeen and this had been her life for a time: she had gotten high, and danced, and had made good friends, and she didn't really have to fuck anyone she didn't want to fuck. The crew of them would fly over country roads in the big, bright cars and shout *Fuck Mississippi* into the summertime nights, and *Fuck Everything*, too. Doing this had felt so good, like a rupturing of the narrative that embalmed them.

Yet she didn't leave. Instead, she just stared at the pile of Van Dorn on the floor, his skin draped in the downcast of television light. She'd been mesmerized by the spot-like scars on his back, nine of them total, and had watched him clench up in sleep as if being kicked. She lit cigarettes, and the little-girl part of her worried about him busting her for smoking. At some point, she had fallen asleep.

"It's your choice," Van Dorn explained the next morning. "I'm not stealing you." He'd been up for hours, having brought coffee and a packet of mini coconut donuts to the room. "You can come home with me. Participate. But it must be your choice."

He'd thought all morning about his invitation, about how to define his hopes. He'd considered trying to explain Samarra—but didn't know how, or even what had happened there. Instead, he confessed to her about losing his twin sister, years before the war. How the siblings had known every single thing about each other, a river of feeling and thought, without words. How he needed so badly to replace this loss, to reinstate this sense of empathy, communion. The death of their closeness was where he'd gone wrong. It was the only time he had ever known peace.

He was terrified Leah would refuse.

She didn't. She didn't say anything, actually, only nodding an okay. She'd felt special, chosen, and had decided right then to do whatever he wanted—for a time, at least. Her only hopes were that he would not hurt her. (She figured he might cause her some pain, but had hoped he would not *damage* her.) None of her friends had come to look for her, anyway.

Within minutes, they were on the road back to Van Dorn's little house, on the bruised-up side of Pitchlynn, Mississippi.

And now.

And now, she was conditioned to his every tic and whim, and she knew she could never leave him. He swore to her that there could be no closer love.

They were twinned, it seemed. There was nothing more to think about.

ODIE LINDSEY'S writing appears in *Best American Short Stories, Iowa Review, Guernica, Electric Literature, Forty Stories: New Writing from Harper Perennial, Fourteen Hills* and elsewhere. A veteran, his related story collection, *We Come To Our Senses*, was recently published by W.W. Norton.

J O H N   B A L A B A N

Back then

Looking for some peace of mind
was like searching for a cricket in a field.
He'd head out, following his best directions
only to drive around from noon to nightfall
past bogs and cornfields and tangly woods.
His car would get stuck, or the battery die
and he would have to hump it to a farmhouse to call for a tow.
Back in town, he would sit at the bar with a beer,
wondering why the locals were lying,
and slapping mosquitoes whining at his ear.
He had all the right gear, just couldn't get there.

One evening he spotted a mule deer
ambling up a hillside path
and he followed it to higher ground
as a huge moon rose off the ridge
where he caught the scent of pine needles.
So he kept on until dark, reaching a ledge
overlooking Phantom Lake and the ghost town,
His breath fogged in the cooling mountain air.
Moonlight seemed to pour from his nostrils.
He made camp there, sleeping that night
in a mess of dreams, troubled with bat squeaks,

with wild burros braying along the nearby creek.
At dawn the bats were pocketed upside down
in the canyon wall rinsed in pink light
and he saw the burros grazing wheatgrass and sage.
At the canyon head, a cave yawned open
but empty of the voices that muttered in the night.
And the blasted tree, high on the mesa rim
—that writhed at dusk like a man crucified—
was a tree again, rocking in the wind.
Stars gone, the sky streaked in sunlight.
A canyon wren, perched in a willow,
plied the dawn with clear, inquiring song.

JOHN BALABAN is the author of twelve books of poetry and prose, including four volumes which together have won The Academy of American Poets' Lamont prize, a National Poetry Series Selection, and two nominations for the National Book Award, After Our War (1974) and Locusts at the Edge of Summer (1998). His *Locusts at the Edge of Summer: New and Selected Poems* won the 1998 William Carlos Williams Award from the Poetry Society of America. Balaban is a director of the Vietnamese Nôm Preservation Foundation and Professor Emeritus of English at North Carolina State University in Raleigh.

BENJAMIN BUSCH

Wilderness

My Commanding Officer was missing. The message came 10 years after our tour in the war. He had retired and was fishing alone on a lake in Canada. Search parties went out. Then he was found.

It's hot as I drive away from home. The funeral will be tomorrow, 737 miles to the cemetery, 11 straight hours. I leave late and head into night, Michigan letting me go. On a route around Toledo, the asphalt is so new the rollers are still parked along the shoulder. Streetlights reflect off the smooth pitch as if it's moist, that oily licorice look of a surface too slick to steer on. I was in charge of repairing roads in Ramadi, filling bomb craters and clearing trash. I never saw a clean street in Iraq, a country where tar is so close to the surface the Sumerians used it as mortar for their bricks.

But that's not what comes to mind right then. I'm already adrift.

It's midnight and my drive is just beginning even though I'm three hours into it. I haven't been to a military burial since 1996. I was only out of the Corps for two months when two birds collided over Camp Lejeune, North Carolina, an attack helicopter rising into a troop transport killing twelve of my Marines. My departure had been so recent, I hadn't even been replaced and my seat in the Sea Knight fell to earth empty. I imagined the fuselage ripped open by Cobra blades, all of us cut to pieces, sky and swamp sprayed with blood. But I was home with my wife trying to see suburban America as a place I could live in.

We bought a small house in College Park, Maryland just inside the beltway and I paced the yard like a pen. I had lost a sense of direction, unable to recognize myself out of uniform. Standing in the honor guard with my peers, my sword drawn, our Dress Blues keeping us stiff, we buried a lieutenant in front of his fiancée. Their wedding was planned for that weekend and friends had all gathered to celebrate. They stood shocked and quiet. There was almost nothing said. It was May. I joined a reserve unit a week later.

I scan the channels for rock stations and they blare in and fizz out, overlapping with talk shows and commercials. A few minutes of AC/DC and then they're gone like their century, signals making their way into space with our casualty reports and radio checks. All of the urgent messages and calls home just noise that passed away.

A sign for the Toledo Zoo stands strange in the dark web of roads and ramps, a conquered hinterland now barren of animals and trees. Before we deployed, my CO named me Lone Wolf because I was often on my own, drawn to the fringe. Our small detachment didn't lose a man in 2005. I was the only one wounded. I remember him rushing into the casualty center as I was attended to. We'd been in Iraq for two weeks then. A decade ago. There's no distance kept in time. It was last month. It was every day, the Euphrates opaque, barely moving past, dense with dust and sewage, no fish striking its surface and no way to see its bed. It boiled, churning rather than flowing, the current indiscernible. No one swam. It was known to pull people under and keep them for miles.

I was sent to swimming lessons for years but found ways to never really learn. I didn't believe it was a physical act I could master and it kept me wary of the pool, where drowning happened. Somehow I remained completely dauntless in the river, the shore always near enough, the current sensible, pressing me, bulging against my waist. The pool was chemical. It burned my eyes and smelled nothing like water.

I failed the swimming merit badge test at Boy Scout camp. We did laps within lanes of roped floats in a deep block of lake. The odd formality of the evaluation returned me to the panic of water taught as danger. I took some in my lungs and coughed myself helpless. Quitting hurt as much as learning I could die in a pond.

The base is still eight hours away but my hair feels long. I may have gone feral since the war, like when I was young. I'm an expatriate returning to Quantico, Virginia where I became a Marine. I spent years there. I think about the zoo, it's absolute captivity. I understand a little how it must be to live in one. All those rules and boundaries and waiting for a gate to be left ajar. It's hard to be an outlier, to get to the outer reaches. It's harder to come back.

An ad hisses for KISS touring later this summer. The first album I ever bought was Love Gun, from a yard sale across the street in Poolville, New York. The cover was incomprehensible and compelling. There was no gun and I didn't understand the innuendo for years. I joined the KISS Army. Then I bought the Destroyer album as another collection was sold. Records were part of garage sales back then, a dollar or two each, especially as guys began buying tapes to play in cars. "Detroit Rock City" was the hit on Destroyer and still plays in southern Michigan all the time. The song ends with a car crash. It comes on at midnight as I drive and the beat takes me back to Poolville, to me before I knew anyone who died. Before war was more than just stories I'd heard. Music takes me to the water.

In the Sangerfield River, which curled around my town, yellow leaves in the stream signaled the end of trout season. Foliage dropped and moved past, suspended and spinning, pressed like scabs onto stones and logs. The river had cooled and I waded through it to the deeper pools where I hoped a worm might still be noticed. I rarely used silver lures, though I had a few. I preferred the hook. I rubbed worms in leaves to marry their scent as if they fell from trees.

I ventured upstream from the ruins of a dam that once powered textile mills and saws. It was fished-out near the village, but no one walked this far up and I considered it undiscovered country. In truth, the area had been well trafficked for two hundred years by boys with poles and men with guns, natives with arrows and nets before that. But I'd never seen any of them. Rediscovered country was almost as good.

As I threw in my line, I tamped the clay bank to form a place to stand in the thinning shadow of an old willow tree. An oak trunk lay below the surface and I had mapped how the water was sucked under, carving a pit patrolled by trout. The bait would have to follow this path or fish would know it to be bait. The river struck its stones, the sound of static between stations, a solitude of water, the hushing of a crowd. I hummed rock songs.

3 AM at a rest stop near Youngstown on the Ohio/Pennsylvania border and people are sleeping in their cars, seats back, windows fogged with air conditioning. The humidity smokes halos around the light poles. Toll plazas are the loneliest places despite people pulling up with their windows rolled down. At this hour the roads are bare. I'm searching for a radio signal and still not thinking of Iraq.

I push past Gettysburg in the dark, markers noting where 50,000 soldiers died, then bend through the Virginias. I shave off my beard in a gas station bathroom. I wonder as I approach the gate to base, if the Marine guard will turn me away. I'm a civilian now. A savage. I look wrong, like a terrorist on my Driver's License. This is tribal territory and I am unrecognizable, my 16 years shorn and starched impossible for him to see in me. I sit straight and want to apologize. I want to confess that I feel less complete now than I did when I belonged here. I'm missing too but no one is looking for me. I'm Lone Wolf. The guard waves me through.

The service is at Eleven Hundred. I have a few minutes to buy a small eagle, globe and anchor pin for my lapel, change into my suit at another gas station and line up at Quantico National Cemetery to follow the hearse, the heat over 100 degrees. I speak of him as my CO, not as a civilian, not as someone who became someone else or was anyone before. Most people wait sealed in their cars, engine fans laboring to keep passengers cool.

Headstones stand in rows draped over the rolling knolls, their perfect geometry revealed and warping as I pass. Someday, if there's anyone left, they'll uncover this cemetery, Arlington too, all the dead in their uniforms, and try to make sense of them. Four hundred thousand and counting, like the terra cotta warriors of Emperor Qin, the fired clay slow to shatter back into silt. We are so quick to be soil, embalmers doing their best to preserve us for…for what? Rediscovery? The pharaohs of Egypt have been uncovered, looted by thieves and archeologists, displayed in museums to be viewed as nothing more than dead. And here's one more, found in a lake at peace. We all go missing when we die. Is it right to find us?

Marines carry the casket to a small brick-pillared committal shelter and we gather around. Only a few make it into the shade, the rest lit bright and squinting. I sweat fast into my black suit, my thick hair dripping at the tips, the sun unavoidable, and I finally think of Iraq. I thought the war would be on my mind the entire trip, but it wasn't. I looked at yellow lines and charcoal hills, tried to stay awake. I wandered and forgot. I had no music in Iraq so I don't return there through songs. I remember Iraq as static.

A priest reads some passages, dust to dust, and no one is invited to say anything about the man in the coffin, the one who survived the war and died fishing alone in a boat. A heart attack. Fell, drowned and drifted for a day, gone wild, lungs filled with lake. He was 58 and two years from receiving military retirement pay. His family will get nothing. Nothing but a plot in a line on a slope. Taps plays its haunting notes. His wife cries quietly. I haven't slept in 28 hours. My suit is soaked.

Then it's over, a line forming to shake hands and offer brief embraces, a folded flag presented to his widow. The day stretches, heat bridging the desert to the hole they have dug. We held memorials in Ramadi for our dead, but we didn't bury them there. They went missing from us, taken away to be laid in graves while patrols went back out, one man short. We're a naval service so every seat in a bird, truck or ship is known as a "boat space". Mine plunged into a swamp without me. They recovered an empty boat on a lake, my CO's watch still in it. That's when they knew. I want to be found alive or never found at all.

At The Basic School, on the far side of base from the cemetery and 23 years ago, we jumped into a pool from a fifteen-foot platform. Full gear. Abandon ship drills. We struck the deep end of the vat with our legs crossed and resurfaced, hands first, splashing furiously above our heads. The purpose was to puncture a hole in imaginary fuel burning above us if our ship had been sunk. These were lessons from World War II. Our backpacks served as life preservers and we kicked our way forward while sweeping the water aside, palms facing out. It seemed absurdist and, though we went about it very seriously, we sputtered and flailed like drunks, lumps of wet woodland camouflage bobbing on packs swollen with clothing in Ziploc bags. It looked like the reenactment of a disaster. Helmets slid over our eyes, rubber rifles hung from our necks and our boots dragged like stones tied to our feet, all of us trying to push the water out of the pool.

I had to come in on days off for remedial instruction in the crawl, which I had already taught myself to do badly, my head up and arms wheeling the way teens escape sharks in movies. The precision of our technique was examined closely. In war, water would be hostile territory, every ship sure to be torpedoed. I wasn't concerned enough that any of this was possible. Lungs full of air, my Dead Man's Float was measured at 11 inches underwater.

I never wore a watch when I was a kid. The sun told the time and I was usually late getting home. I never worried, like my parents did, about drowning. In the bright noon I tied a wet maple leaf by its stem eight inches above the hook to serve as a sail. It joined the swirling camouflage. Filament pulled over my finger from the reel so I could feel the action. I was stalking while standing still, almost holding my breath, the line unwinding. Leaves trapped in the flow pressed under the fallen oak and surged on the other side as if spilling up from beneath the earth. My pilot leaf was lost in the billowing wreckage, uniquely indistinguishable, and the line went lax as the bait circled the pool. I can see myself then, hunched on the shore watching the reflection, waiting for the dull golden flash of a trout strike, hunting the frontier. Being there in the sounds of fall, I was in the space that still grows around solitude. My CO found this one last place, heard the call of the wild, listened to the water, went all the way.

I drive on as dirt is shoveled over him, through *The Wilderness* battlefield and find it noted only by a plaque. It's strange to see a sign beside wilderness that says it's wilderness. Like a sign in a city for a zoo. They still find bones here, men forever lost in the woods. The radio is on but I'm afloat on the road, forest on one side, the Euphrates on the other, past ads for caves cut open for tourists, squares of pasture and lawn, all the found places marked, fenced and named, rain dropping so thick people are pulling over, the highway ahead blurring into cloud. I think of the funeral as the sound pounds the windshield and roof. Rest in peace, sir. I want to know what the water told you.

BENJAMIN BUSCH is a writer, filmmaker, and illustrator. He's the author of the memoir *Dust to Dust* (Ecco) and his essays have arrived in *Harper's*, *The New York Times Magazine* and on NPR. His poems have appeared in *North American Review, Prairie Schooner, Five Points, Michigan Quarterly*

Review and *Epiphany,* among others. He teaches nonfiction for the low-residency MFA in Creative Writing program at Sierra Nevada College, Tahoe, and lives on a farm in Michigan where he shovels by day and writes at night.

STEVE MUMFORD

Artist Statement

I went to Iraq for the first time in late April, 2003, just after the US invasion, as a civilian artist. I wanted to document whatever I could see of the 'war on terror', although at that time the war was considered over by most of the troops and the Iraqis I met. This would change over the next six months, particularly in Baghdad and Anbar Province, and I continued to record this change in drawings during six trips to Iraq up until 2008, and two to Afghanistan during Obama's surge.

In Baghdad I got to know a group of Iraqi artists and writers. They introduced me to their favorite gathering spots and gave me some of their perspective on that conflict.

I drew veterans recovering from their combat wounds at Walter Reed Army Hospital and Brook Army Medical Center. I drew the daily routine of doctors, nurses and occasional carnage at the Baghdad ER.

I drew usually directly from life, either on my own in Baghdad (where I lived in hotels and apartments) and other cities, or embedded with US military units. Much of what I saw was life lived with dignity under minor and occasionally major duress. Sometimes actually finding the war was difficult due to its random nature; I often heard bombs detonating distantly, rarely near me. Iraqis and US soldiers alike carried on with their routine tasks with barely a grumble.

Back from the war I painted larger works in which I tried to distill the deeper meaning of my experiences and my feelings about the soldiers and their war. I continue this project, showing my work at Postmasters Gallery in NYC.

I've also drawn in Gitmo, along the Louisiana coastline during the BP oil spill, and at some of President Trump's campaign rallies for *Harper's Magazine*.

CSH 4686

Ramadi

047

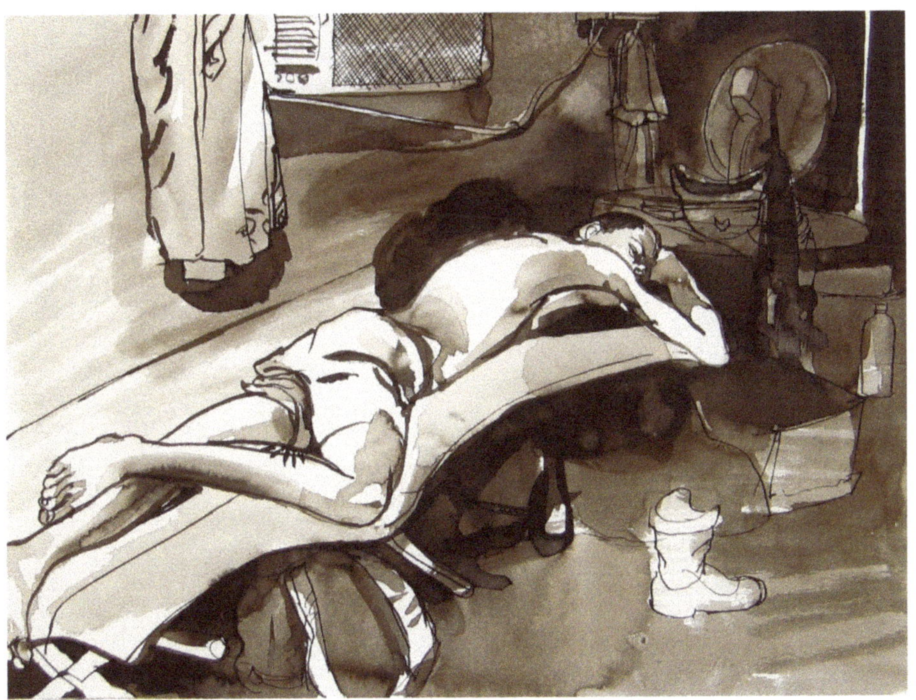

Pritsolas

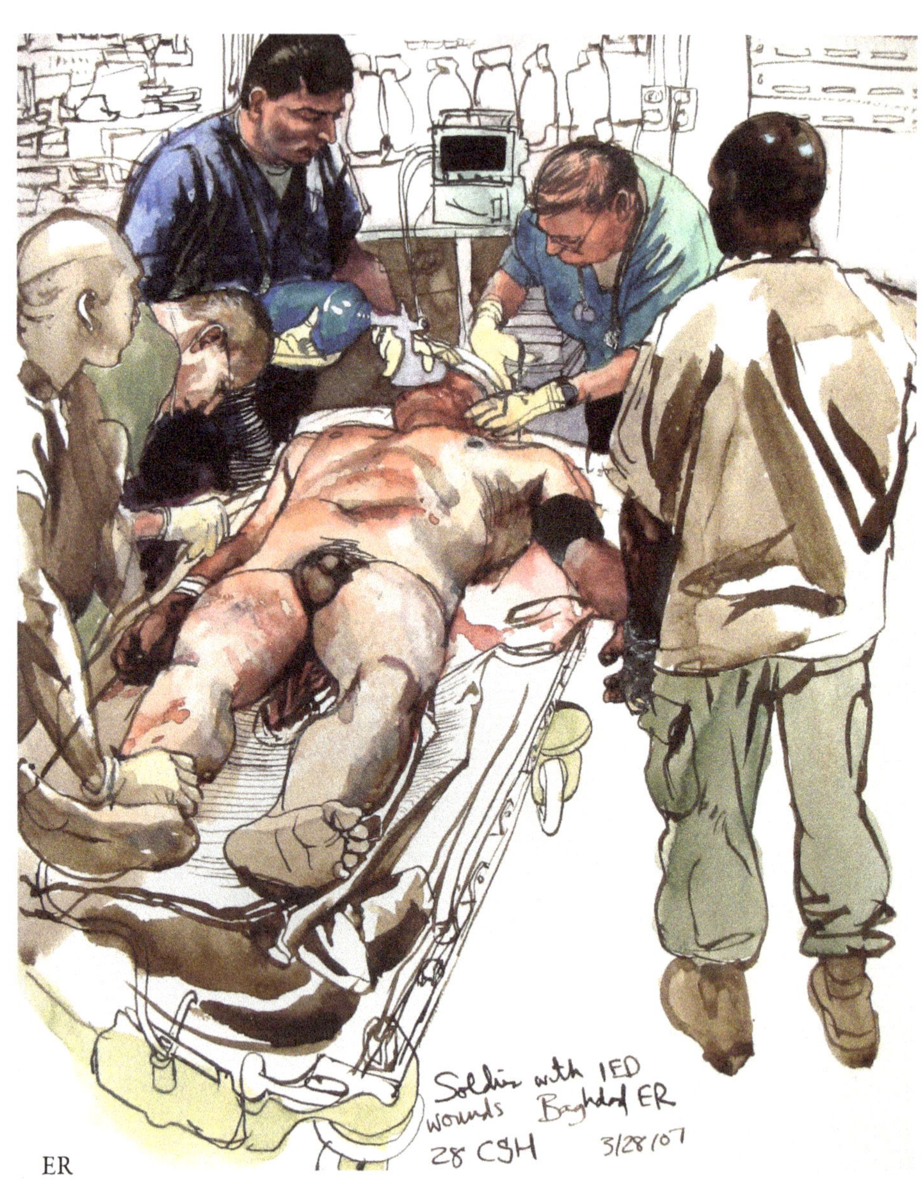

Soldier with IED
wounds Baghdad ER
28 CSH   3/28/07
ER

CHRISTIAN KIEFER

Golden Silence of the Heart

The realization that he was free of it, free of it all, had come to him so slowly that had he not lived to the age of ninety, year of our Lord 1880, he might not have understood it at all, the memory in some ways still stronger than anything to come after and yet the sum total of those years of peace and relative happiness ultimately outstripping the grim violent time to come before, those ten years that started before Austerlitz and ended at Waterloo, a period of time so distant to him now that in some ways the whole experience seemed but remnants of a story he had been told by someone else, someone who had been there and had survived and had returned home, scarred and shaking, already an old man at the age of twenty-four, breaking down in odd moments for many years thereafter even though everything about his life had changed, first through the fact that the war itself was over and then through marriage and children came and later grandchildren and even greatgrandchildren, the long incredible genealogy he had fostered presenting itself as a kind of marvel even more striking than the changes to the land itself, changes that he could never have imagined, not even as a young man filled with dreams about what he might become or in the storm and tumult of Napoleon's speeches, for despite everything, his dull hatred for the man who had taken him from his home to fight in a conflict against people who spoke not the emperor's language but his own, despite this and the hardships and privations of an army ever on the move, he could not help but feel his embarrassed and recalcitrant heart swing up into the rhetoric, from the sulfurous dirt in which he stood with his companions to some bright starlit future, and yet now he was in that future and the emperor was not, his own ability simply to *not die* having outlived the tiny tyrant by fifty-nine years, eight years longer than that man had himself walked upon the surface of the earth, a thought that gave him some sense of accomplishment at least, that he had outdone the very creature who had threatened his life by dint of a war that even now he could hardly understand, a war that did not, in the end, take his life, but took instead the lives of his brothers, the first going to ground in the days just after Austerlitz and the two others, older than he himself had been, although that point seemed moot now, killed on the battlefields of Raszyn so that he returned to Waldkirch an only child, making for the small home in which he had spent his childhood because he did not know what else to do, his entire life having seemed, now, a waste of time, drafted when he was fifteen at the behest of their new king and told to fight for Napoleon and then told, in the fall of 1813, that his country had switched sides and was now allied with Prussia and the Austrian Empire so that his three brothers had now, by royal decree, perished fighting for the enemy, a decree that felt like a hot knife held to his heart but which his parents seemed to take in stride, telling him, simply and quietly, that God giveth and God taketh away, words that did little to douse his anger and frustration in understanding that he had been born into a world that felt not like what Jesus promised but instead like the upturned stump upon which his father, and later his brothers, and later still he himself, had slaughtered various small animals—wood grouse and hare and the occasional fox—its surface black and slick and buzzing with flies, that world a world in which he could not find the hatchet but knew it was always there, hanging just above the killing stump and that there was nothing he could do about it at all, the years passing and his occasional homecoming during brief respites offering only a sense that something else besides war was still possible in the world, although the crackle of gunfire and the low thump of the twelve pounders seemed to ride in his chest even when they were silent, the days and nights punctuated then by a strange desire to hear them again, as if in hearing them he might somehow silence their ghosts, so when he was called up again and again and again, in his secret heart there had always been a thread of relief, although he knew it could not go on forever and when at last it did, indeed, come to a close at Waterloo, he returned to his parents' home in the forest feeling as if the ghosts of those guns would crackle and thump forever in his dreams, and yet even that was not to be, for time passed and although he was not a young man anymore—fifteen in 1806 at Austerlitz and twenty-four at Waterloo—he was experiencing what he thought of as a young man's desires, for he had met, in the French city of Troyes, in 1814, a young woman who, like the low thumps of the twelve-pounders, he could not seem to forget, and so, in the winter of the year he had returned home he left it once more, setting off for the French countryside, an errand he knew would be fruitless, for how could she possibly remember him after all that had happened, not only to him but to her, and in his heart he knew that she would likely have married another, for how could she have done otherwise when there was no world in which he was cared for in any way, the whole of it malevolent and heartbreaking from first breath to last, and yet when he arrived in Troyes, his resources already having dwindled to crumbs, she was waiting for him, had been waiting for him, in her way, for a full year, especially after word of Napoleon's defeat had come from the capital, for she knew then that his return to Troyes was at least possible, although she also understood that he would need to cross most of the known world to reach her and yet he had come and she was there for him and they were married soon thereafter and soon enough the first of their children was toddling about the town, speaking not German but French, since in the end he settled there in her village rather than bringing her back to his, it seeming easier that way for he was, after all, already present in Troyes and her parents and family were there and while he lamented leaving his parents alone back in the Schwarzwald, he knew that after everything he had done and been through and survived, he could hardly return to that shadowy forest with its staggering trees and dark pathways, the thought of it alone bringing his skin to gooseflesh which his new bride, young and pink and as lovely as the French sunshine, kissed away, something she would do for him even as the years passed and their brood increased, the children coming and growing and taking wives and husbands of their own, the fact that he raised, after everything that had happened to him, a French family continuing to be a kind of marvel, something he was both embarrassed by and proud of, as if in changing their nationality he had changed himself, and maybe, in fact he had, for at some point during that long stretch of years he realized that the ghost sounds of that war had faded from his dreams until they were hardly audible at all, a fact that he learned only after his beloved took her last breath at the age of sixty-eight in the year 1856, that day so bright and warm that the salt of his sweat mixed with the salt of his tears, the sense of absence so great that he might have tottered into the hole after her had his oldest daughter's arm not come through his own, and his oldest son's on the opposite side so that when he looked up it her eyes staring back at him, her gaze in all of theirs, filled with despair and loss but also with love and with a silence he could use fill the gap she had left behind, a gap which he knew had once contained the guns and the twelve-pounders and which he could feel, even now, even standing at her grave, was being filled by his family in a moment which he thought would last only a few months or years but which seemed to stretch on and on toward the end of the century, not one year or two or ten but twenty four, a number of years to match the age he had been when he had first come for her hand sixty-six years before, and although those last decades of his life—near two and a half of them—held occasional moments of terrible loneliness, what he remembered most of all, at the end, was that he was surrounded by her memory in everything that remained and continued to remained, not dying but living with all the shine of those mornings when he had awakened with her by his side, oh oh oh God how he would have loved to tell her such a thing, that she had saved him and that she was saving him still, that all he had ever needed was silence and she had given it to him and had given it, in trust, to their children and their grandchildren and their greatgrandchildren, a kind of golden soundlessness that he might not even have been able to identify but which, he knew now, was like a kind of boat to buoy the heart over the biggest of the waves.

———————

CHRISTIAN KIEFER earned his Ph.D. in American literature from the University of California, Davis, and is on the English faculty of American River College in Sacramento. He is an active poet, songwriter, and recording artist, and lives in the foothills of the Sierra Nevada Mountains in Northern California with his wife and six sons. He is the author of the novels *The Animals* and *The Infinite Tides* and the novella, *One Day Soon Time Will Have No Place Left to Hide*.

ANDRIA WILLIAMS

A Legacy

Leo Szilard was the Hungarian-born physicist who conceived the nuclear chain reaction. One of the primary scientists on the Manhattan Project, he became strongly opposed to the bomb's use against civilians and spent the last months of WWII in a bitter battle against the U.S. government, urging the new Truman administration to publicly demonstrate the bomb's power first before dropping it on a Japanese city.

In the bedroom mirror you tighten your tie, button your cufflinks, comb back your dark salt-and-pepper hair with a series of short swoops. You turned forty-seven two months ago and realized all at once that you look exactly like the half-dozen great-uncles who stared out at you from small oval frames in your parents' dim, wallpapered hallway back in Budapest decades ago. You used to stick your tongue out at them as you stomped to your childhood bedroom in shorts and suspenders. Now here you are with the same soft jowl, slumped little mouth, oversized, worried-looking eyes. Funny how time works, a person is so young and then suddenly old.

If one is given the opportunity to get old, Trude would probably say. She is a doctor, this is how she thinks. A woman of undiluted intelligence, she debates you even in your head, and she is always right. You are both lucky to be growing older, the two of you having escaped Nazi Berlin, separately, by the skin of your teeth, in '33, at the time close friends and sometime lovers. The physician and the physicist, you are perhaps an unlikely pair, but you are also (you like to think) ideally suited. You've always lived separately, with long regular visits, because you both need privacy for your work, and because you like the being-apart -- a gleeful freedom that turns to pining like teenagers -- and the coming-back-together. Her opinion of you matters very highly, sometimes to the point of your distraction. She has the brains and the beauty: tall and long-armed and strong, her silver-streaked hair in a high, fluffy bun, no makeup, you can picture her, her lovely neck, delicious elbows – and you with your old-man face now, it's enough to make you laugh; your puppy-dog eyes, your crooked nose--

But no matter; you were not hired on to the University of Chicago and now the Manhattan Project for your looks. You chuckle at this little joke and think you should write it to Trude in a letter: *I'm afraid they regret hiring me for my looks.* She would find that funny.

I am sure some of them do regret hiring you, she would say, with a twist of affection to her mouth but a voice turning serious. She means the five years you've spent on the project and your desperation, now, to keep the military from using it.

Trude knows the basics of what you are building – what, now, you have just finished. She is not the only one: Oppenheimer's wife knows, Wilson's wife knows. But she calls it "the project," has never said the word "bomb," and what the wives know of it is only a fraction of how devastating it will really be.

Which is why you became so upset, last night on the telephone, when she suggested in exhaustion that you stop fighting President Truman and that dybbuk of his, Leslie Groves, head of the Project, who's tried to get you interned as an enemy for the duration of the war. Truman and Groves want to drop the bomb on Japan in less than a month; you oppose this with every fiber of your being. In letter after letter to the brand-new President -- a country bumpkin with the scientific insights of a ten-year-old – you've written that the bomb's use would be immoral, that there is no excuse for a civilized and moral nation to annihilate eighty thousand civilians with one stroke. America has an "obligation of restraint," you wrote , "and if we were to violate this obligation, our moral position would be weakened in the eyes of the world and in our own eyes."

You know I agree with you, Trude said. But you are working yourself into constant agitation. You can't control the military or the President. Perhaps it's time to stop fighting them-

Stop fighting them? you'd cried. I've got sixty-eight other scientists who've put their names on paper saying there is no need to use it. There are other things we can do. We can test it publicly. We can offer Japan a detailed terms of surrender first, before we use this weapon on old people and babies. Sixty-nine scientists saying not to use it and they listen to the four patsies who agree with them--

Then, you stopped talking. Her end of the line was silent. She had heard all this before and besides, you were proving her point.

You said, I am sorry I raised my voice at you.

She had sighed, lightly. *Oytser -- sweetheart -- there is only so much you can do. Maybe this is the price we pay for peace.*

You hadn't argued any more. The call ended pleasantly a few minutes later. You wished she would appear beside you, tap your crooked nose and laugh at another of your silly jokes. But you couldn't think of another joke to make. And you knew that this was not about peace.

You do not want to toot your own horn, as the Americans like to say, but the germ of the project started at least in part with you, when the possibility of a nuclear chain reaction came into your mind on a Southampton street corner in 1933, right after you'd fled Berlin. For six years you'd kept your theory close to the bone. If Hitler got hold of the science, it would be the biggest disaster mankind had ever seen. It was you who wrote to FDR, told him the U.S. must do everything within its power to achieve a nuclear weapon before the Germans did. Einstein's name was on the letter, yes, but you wrote it.

One scientist after another fled Nazi Europe for America, and suddenly there you all were together, a meeting of great minds driven by an urgency none of you had ever known before: working day and night, sharing notes, solving problems that would ordinarily have taken four times as long. Feet to the fire: Heisenberg, after all, was still in Hitler's Germany, making his own calculations, and in the end he would not be off by much. The whole world at stake. A ghastly time for millions, but – you could not deny it, none of the scientists would have denied it -- the most exciting time of your life. Everyone swept up in it.

And you beat the Germans. You beat everybody. In 1944, when it became clear that the war would be won long before Hitler could ever acquire such a weapon, Joseph Rotblat, the brilliant Pole, pulled out of the project. *We've defeated Hitler, we've met our goal,* he said. Then he looked you in the eye: *Haven't we?*

But you stayed on and worked as feverishly as before.

I think it's more about the Soviets, Rotblat warned, a few days before he left, over coffee at your kitchen table. *That's why they want to drop it. They want to show Stalin what they can do.*

You'd hemmed and hawed, said, *We don't know that.*

Japan will fall very soon and we don't need to kill hundreds of thousands of civilians to make her do it. It's a devil of a way to show off, Rotblat had said, *killing women and children. A devil of a pissing contest.* He rubbed his forehead, made a small disgusted sound, looked off to one side.

After he left, you poured yourself another cup of coffee, added a splash of cream. The white dollop hit the bottom of the small mug and bloomed upward into a flower, unfurling. You were angry at Rotblat for disturbing the air in your own, cozy apartment. You were angry because he was right. Your stomach clenched and you tossed the beige liquid down the sink. From that day on you took your coffee black.

Why did you stay on when others, like Rotblat, had left? What were you hoping to accomplish, to gain?

Trude has never asked you. You hope she never will.

The threat you'd joined up to fight was gone. Why did you stay on?

Why did you stay on?

The day the bomb is dropped, you sit at home. You are alone. It is a beautiful day in August, the 6th, the high point of an American summer. Children are free to romp at their town's pool, to cannonball into the water again and again, to fish by quiet ponds, to ride bikes on new pavement.

Now the bomb has hit, and on the other side of the world, eighty thousand Japanese are dead. Blasted into vapor, or peeled like peaches. Women, children, babies, pets. Elderly couples. Their jokes, stories, imaginations, vanished just like that. The way a certain man walked with a light shuffle, the way a woman tucked her hair behind an ear: gestures, the myriad types of laughter, the odd and particular games of individual children. The weight of what their minds and hearts held.

You know the death toll will more than double.

The phone rings and rings.

Truman announces the success from a ship at sea: "We've spent 2 billion dollars on the greatest scientific gamble in history—and won." You write to Trude – you cannot yet call-- "He offends my sense of proportion."

You live almost two decades after that; you and Trude finally marry.

For the rest of your life, you work for nuclear arms control. With Einstein, you form the Emergency Committee of Atomic Scientists. You move to D.C. to advise Kennedy; you publicly oppose the hydrogen bomb; you try to form a hot-line for Soviet and American officials, any last-ditch intervention that could prevent nuclear war. You leave physics and turn instead to biology, which suits you. In time you'll be known as the inventor of the chemostat, which allows bacterial cultures to be produced continually; you publish a theory of aging and a method for cloning mammalian cells. You become a fellow at the Salk Center and move to San Diego, a place so beautiful it seems no one can actually deserve to live there.

When, later in life, you are diagnosed with bladder cancer, you cure it with a radiation program you designed yourself, a technology that will continue to be used for others.

You have brought good to this world, Trude reminds you, from time to time, on evening walks when you grow moody. You don't entirely believe her but you don't feel like quarreling; the quiet slosh of your urine bag – you are still finishing the radiation treatments – is answer enough for the grimness you feel. (When one of those shirtless teenage beach bums strolls by, you raise your coat hem slightly and slosh the bag at him, feeling devilish, as if to say See what awaits you, young man. His eyes widen, his glorious pectorals contract as he sidesteps off the curb. Trude says, "Leo, stop, that's perverse.")

She knows you think about the bomb. It pains her, which both troubles you and, on your lesser days, brings you a small, strange satisfaction.

But she doesn't know how *often* it crosses your mind. Some days, forty times. Fifty times. Other days merely ten or twelve. It comes to you in flashes, images: the cloud, the spread, the falling buildings. The people lingering in hospitals for days or months, their eyes bandaged, skin flowered with sarcomas or badly burned, fetus-pink, stretched and seeping. Children with their wrists curled under. The garden of horrors you helped cultivate and bring to this earth. You do not want this to be your legacy, but what else can it be?

In La Jolla, the sun-warmed town where you will both eventually die, you'll catch a glimpse of Trude's bare arm, tan, muscles flexing, as she plants her succulents, and shudder to imagine its smoothness bubbled from below like lava on island rock. You'll think of a cancer blooming in her belly like some sea creature, fanning slowly, scalloped edges.

Some days, you are almost envious of victimhood, the purity of it. You are stupid enough to mention this to Trude, only once, and she slaps your arm so hard it surprises both of you. *You could have stayed in Berlin in 1933 if you wanted a taste of victimhood,* she says, her voice nearly a snarl. *You could have seen how great it is, how about that.*

I'm sorry, Trude. I didn't mean it.

You'll think how angry you would feel if it were her killed in that blast. You'd be beside yourself, you'd feel furious and robbed. You know it would make you want to take things from other people, again and again, every day of your life. But also you know that would solve nothing. People can take and take, and they always do; but they can never take back.

Trude comes in from the garden, smelling like sage. There is a dry nub of lavender in her hair and dirt on her chin. You wish you'd known then that she would outlive you by seventeen years; every lover who'll die first should have that knowledge, you think, and keep the secret to themselves, a mercy. When your heart stops the following evening she will not be able to revive you and that will be that. She will devote herself to your papers and deliver them to the local University, where she will give a small lecture on your accomplishments, point to a photo of Lunar Crater Szilard that has been named for you (formerly Crater 116), of which she is proud, though it is heavily worn and cannot be seen from Earth.

She stoops to pick up a sprig she has dropped and stands with a tiny groan.

I think we are finally old, she laughs.

You want to smile at her, but you can't quite. You are not as old as some, but you are older than many.

————

ANDRIA WILLIAMS is the author of the novel *The Longest Night* (Random House, 2016) and editor of the *Military Spouse Book Review* (www.militaryspousebookreview.com). She is currently at work on a second novel.

SJ SINDU

Fundraising

The tsunami brought peace to Toronto. Almost everyone I knew had lost somebody—to the waters, to the chaos, or just to the unknowing. My mother sat next to the phone all day, waiting for a call. Kannan told me that his mother was no different. Even we boys felt lethargic. No one could get the energy to fight, or even to patrol the neighborhood. The other gangs were the same, if Toronto news was anything to go by. A rare ceasefire, news outlets were calling it, a brief bout of peace on the dangerous streets of Scarborough.

Most days we sat catatonic on Kannan's couch, not knowing what to do, watching the BBC's coverage of Sri Lanka.

"What we need is cash," Kannan said.

A news anchor with shiny blonde hair was telling us that the Sri Lankan government had asked for foreign aid.

"Those assholes are never going to give the money to Tamils," Kannan said. By assholes, he meant the Sri Lankan government.

We nodded. We knew this was true. We also knew that most foreign donations weren't cash—clothes that were too scandalous for the Sri Lankan women to wear, toys that weren't important enough to distribute, electronics that wouldn't work without a transformer—and all these things were gathering dust in warehouses and clogging up the shipping and transport systems. Any money would line the pockets of the Sri Lankan president and his family. Some of it would go to helping relief efforts in the Sinhalese areas. None of it would be for Tamil people.

"We should raise money," Kannan said. "We're good at that."

We nodded, but no one moved, no one said anything. For a week we'd been watching footage of bodies streaming down flooded streets, temples cracked open like coconuts, cement wells pushed up out of the ground and lying on their sides in the sand. Next to this ruthless nature, our daily violences of gang life looked small and petty.

Kannan's grandmother hobbled into the room.

"I made tea," she said.

She shooed Kannan into the kitchen to pour us tea in small ceramic cups.

"You young people should be doing something." She gestured at the TV. "They need cash, not viewers."

So we started to raise money. We took investments from Tamil businesses in Scarborough to lift up the people back home. At Muthu's DVDs and Music, the owner refused to donate anything.

"You're thugs," he said. "Nothing more than boys." He spit on the ground.

This was as per usual. Kannan nodded to me, as usual, and I, as usual, pushed a pistol into the owner's gut, which, as usual, was enough to convince him. Sometimes, to make a point, we made people give us double the usual.

We posted up near the Hindu temple in Richmond and stopped the women going in and out. We demanded their gold jewelry.

"This is for the Tamils back home," we said. "Think of them. Your prayers are worth nothing if you don't contribute."

They handed us their gold chains, pulled the bangles off their wrists, unscrewed their heavy earrings.

"Thank you," we said.

When they were gone, we sorted the jewelry in the van: real gold and costume jewelry. The costume jewelry pile was three times as large.

"Those old hags," Kannan said. He put his face in his hands and laughed.

At the end of the week, we'd only raised five thousand dollars. And so Kannan called his guy, who called another guy, who called another, and a few hours later, a car pulled up in front of Kannan's apartment building with one pound of pure cocaine.

Problem was, we had no idea how to cut or sell coke. Coke was the Jamaican gang's thing. We went to the corners of Jane and Finch, where they sold. That was our territory, but we'd always had an alliance saying they could sell here, since police ignored the area. But now here we were, about to ask them to teach us how to get in on their biggest moneymaker.

There were four of us plus Kannan, and only three Jamaican boys, one on our side of the street and two across the way. Kannan approached the bald Jamaican boy leaning with his foot up on the side of a covered bus stop.

"Where's Jay-Jay?" Kannan asked.

We all held our guns close under our heavy winter jackets.

"Fuck you," the boy said. He watched the cars passing instead of us.

Kannan stepped up to him, pulling back his jacket to show his gun. "You're on our turf, blackie. We need to talk to Jay-Jay."

The boy fingered his own gun behind his back. "Jay-Jay got moved."

I tapped Kannan on the elbow, which was our code that he needed to calm down. He zipped his jacket back up.

"We need to talk to Jay-Jay," he said.

The boy took out his phone and dialed someone. He talked in a fast dialect I couldn't catch, hung up, and said, "Jay-Jay's coming."

We waited, us and the Jamaican boys. We all watched each other and no one moved.

A half hour later, a car pulled up and Jay-Jay got out—a tiny, dark man with a lopsided afro.

He greeted Kannan with a handshake. "This must be important," he said. They'd been friends once, back in seventh grade.

"We're raising money for the tsunami victims," Kannan said. "We need your boys to train our boys on how to cut and sell."

The bald boy who'd been the first one at the bus stop got up in Kannan's face. "You don't need shit," he said.

Kannan pushed him back.

The boy roared and rushed at Kannan, but Jay-Jay got in the way.

"Calm the fuck down," Jay-Jay said.

But Kannan kept pushing the boy, pushing and pushing until Jay-Jay drew his gun.

Before he could even aim, Kannan grabbed ahold of Jay-Jay's head and slammed him down onto the concrete. The boy, too shocked to respond, backed himself into the corner of the glass bus stop.

Kannan kneeled next to Jay-Jay. We held our breaths until the blood leaked out of Jay-Jay's head, and then we ran, scattered like leaves.

Later that day, we sat in Kannan's living room and watched BBC coverage of the tsunami.

Kannan's grandmother brought out tea in little mismatched cups for everyone. I drank mine in a glass that had yellow flowers on it, trying not to let my hand shake too much.

"How did your fundraising go?" she asked.

We all watched Kannan, waited.

"Not good enough," Kannan said.

She patted his arm. "You'll do better next time," she said.

When she was gone, Kannan said to me, "I want one of you posted in this building at all hours. And double up the gun stock in my room." He closed his eyes and I guessed he was seeing Jay-Jay on the ground. "This peace won't last."

———————

SJ SINDU'S debut novel, *Marriage of a Thousand Lies*, is forthcoming in 2017 from Soho Press. She was a 2013 Lambda Literary Fellow and her hybrid fiction and nonfiction chapbook, *I Once Met You But You Were Dead*, was the winner of the 2016 Split Lip Turnbuckle Chapbook Contest. Sindu's creative writing has appeared or is forthcoming in *Brevity, The Normal School, The Los Angeles Review of Books, apt, Vinyl Poetry, PRISM International, Fifth Wednesday Journal, rkvry quarterly*, and elsewhere.

STEVEN CHURCH

Hit List[1]

These people haven't heard heavy metal. They can't take it. If you play it for 24 hours, your brain and body functions start to slide, your train of thought slows down and your will is broken. That's when we come in and talk to them.

--Sergeant Mark Hadsell, of Psy Ops, to Newsweek magazine

Metallica: "Enter Sandman"

There was a time in the late 80's—a decade still tinged with the sepia tones of nostalgia for me—when the only tape in the Kenwood tape-deck in my 79 Mazda RX-7 was Metallica's *And Justice for All* playing on an eternal loop. Not because my tape deck was broken. Not because I didn't have other tapes. Just because I loved it. The album meant something. *And Justice* came before the *Black Album* featuring "Enter Sandman" and was the first album recorded without their original bass player, Cliff, who was killed when a tour bus rolled over on him. Later the "dude who replaced Cliff," (aka Jason Newsted) would complain bitterly that Lars and James turned the bass way down on *And Justice*, de-emphasizing his tracks to the point of near inaudibility, a

---

1 http://www.guardian.co.uk/music/2008/dec/11/gunsnroses-elvis-presley-human-rights

possible metaphor for the loss they all felt so deeply—the loss of Cliff and his gut-ripping bass riffs—or maybe just evidence, as Jason suggested, that Lars, the son of a professional tennis player, was a control freak in running shorts who didn't trust him to handle the job. None of this mattered to me. I just loved the noise. *And Justice* was also the first album for which Metallica created a MTV video, and they used it to showcase their radio-friendly ballad, One—a very popular video about an angst-ridden mummy . . . or something like that (OK, so it's based on the Dalton Trumbo anti-war novel, *Johny Get Your Gun*, and not my favorite song on the album, but still a visually arresting and compelling video that probably won awards.) *And Justice* was, by most accounts, their first "commercially viable" record and, by many other accounts, the beginning of a downhill slide. But I didn't care. I loved the album deeply and passionately. I listened to *And Justice* in the morning, on the way to work, during my lunch break, and after basketball practice, on the way home for dinner. I listened to *And Justice* while smoking dope, drinking Mickey's Big Mouths, and fucking my nymphomaniac girlfriend out at a campground by the lake, my bony teenage hips pumping and banging like a piston to the rhythm of driving guitar. When friends rode in my car, they complained about the noise and teased me, demanding another tape, something else, anything but the same damn songs. But I didn't care. Some mornings as I pulled into the parking lot of Lawrence High School, home of the Chesty Lions (seriously, that's the mascot), I'd crank up "Dire Maker," lean my head back and feel the soft brush of my mullet hair-do on the back of my neck as I screamed along with James Hetfield, "Dear Mother, Dear Father/What is this hell you have put me through?" because I was a teenage boy, riddled with angst and because it felt good. Not because it meant anything, not because my parents had put me through any kind of hell, really, besides the usual 80's divorce. But the raw emotional truth is that I loved Metallica[2]. I needed it. I needed

---

2 I attended my first live Metallica concert a few years ago at our local soulless sports arena in Fresno (a place named after a grocery chain) where I was inducted into what lead vocalist, James Hetfield called, "the Metallica Family," which as far as I could tell looked eerily like a Promise Keepers rally—almost entirely male, overweight, chanting and swaying to monotonous rhythms, many of them occasionally bursting out in ecstatic fits, yelling "Yessssss!" at the top of their lungs or the joyous, "Whoooooooo."—the major difference between the two groups being that everyone in the Family wore black instead of khaki Dockers and yellow t-shirts, and many of them had interesting facial hair, piercings, and sleeve tattoos. Oh, and they were blasting Metallica at full gut-rumbling volume. I felt like I was standing inside a jet engine . . . Aside from that, the place did feel a lot like a church—perhaps one of those pentacostal, apocalyptic ones where they preach about the End Times, blast rock music, drink strychnine and handle rattlesnakes. The environment was ecstatic, positively epiphanic at times. And when Metallica played "Enter Sandman" all the Family members went completely apeshit crazy and began pumping their arms into the air, 15,000 fists thrusting in unison and all of them chanting, "Enter night. Exit light. Off to never-neverland," at the top of their lungs. It was a little frightening, even for someone who was sympathetic to the Metallica Family values. Everyone knew all the words to Enter Sandman and every single person sang those words, often while clutching a cup of liquid in one hand that might as well have been strychnine, and raising the other in the air, eyes closed in a silent sort of revery, lost in the spiritual wash of noise. At times, throughout the show, James would fall silent himself and let the audience sing the chorus to a particular song. It was like the call-and-response I've seen between preachers and their audience. Like most born-agains, the audience knew the stuff from *And Justice* and the rest of the band's *New Testament* but had a harder time with lessons from the older books of the

the sound, the noise and the odd feeling of peace and calm that washed over me when I listened. Some mornings I just wanted to skip school, skip basketball practice, and hide inside all that window-rattling, chest-humming, ear-ringing noise of power-chord metal on full volume. I wanted to stay in the car, letting the sound roll over me, drown in it and pretend that I didn't hate high school or myself or my nymphomaniac girlfriend. And maybe that's where the meaning is—in the escape, the out of body sort of rush, that feeling of being enveloped. Wrapped in noise. Comforted. Like sound therapy. And maybe the meaning of it is only in that moment, trapped forever in those interstices between spaces, between home and high school, car and classroom, past and present.

Metallica canon, albums like *Kill 'Em All*, *Ride the Lightning*, and *Master of Puppets*. As much as I liked And Justice, I'm really more of an "old school" Metallica fan these days—reveling in the messy angst and fucked up time-signatures of "Seek and Destroy" from their first album. As with most old testaments these books are darker and full of pestilence and smite. Kill Em All features songs like "Seek and Destroy," "Metal Militia," "No Remorse," and "The Four Horsemen." Despite an edge of its own, And Justice is an album mostly about social justice, the environment, and mental health. But *The Black Album*, which followed *And Justice for All*, featuring "Enter Sandman," was by far the band's most hit-heavy, radio-friendly album and the most popular track, "Enter Sandman," the very song that sent the Metallica Family masses into near hysterical worship is, in my opinion, also perhaps one of the silliest and most ridiculous songs the band has ever recorded. It features, after all, an almost sing-song chorus based a nursery rhyme and alluding to the children's classic, Peter Pan (which, I would argue, is markedly different from the creepy Oompa-loompa-esque chanting in "Frayed Ends of Sanity" on And Justice). If you try, you can sing most of "Enter Sandman" like a nursery rhyme. Try it. Try to hear the soft melody of, "Exit light. Enter night. Take my hand. Off to never never land," and now imagine it, accompanied by gut-ripping guitar riffs, played over and over and over again, all night long.

2. Sesame Street: "Sunny Day" theme song:

sunny days. sweeping the clouds away. on my way, to where the air is sweet. can you tell me how to get how to get to sesame street? come and play. everything's a-okay. family neighbors friends. iraqi. that's where we meet. can you tell me how to get, how to get to . . . sunny days. sweeping the clouds away. on my way to where the air is sweet. can you tell me how to get, how to get to sesame street? come and play. everything's a-okay. family neighbors friends. detainee. that's where we meet. can you tell me how to get, how to get to sesame street, how to get to sesame street, how to get to sesame street, how to get to sesame street? And what happens when we get there? What happens when the nostalgic weight of our memories, our love for songs and giant stuffed birds or invisible woolly Mammoths, meets the immovable fact: we torture to a soundtrack. We torture to the Sesame Street theme song. This happens. At detention centers around the world. We (you, me, our country) use music to psychologically break prisoners and detainees. Much of it is music you and I know and love. Much of it is metal. But some is music from your childhood, weaponized and deployed strategically. Music like "Sunny Day," the Sesame Street theme song.

3. Guns N' Roses: "Welcome to the Jungle"

Welcome to the Jungle was one of many rock songs used by Task Force Ranger during the invasion of Panama (Operation Just Cause) in 1989 in an effort to drive Manuel Noriega from power and then roust him from the Vatican Embassy in Panama City. The military set up massive loudspeakers outside the building and blasted music 24 hours a day. In addition to Guns N' Roses, they played a lot of Elvis Presley, Bruce Springsteen, and many of the same favorite songs used against prisoners today. At night they bathed the building in ultra-bright light, haunting him with eternal day, making it nearly impossible for him to get some sleep or a simple moment of quiet peace.

When my son, Malcolm was still in diapers, just learning to talk, he used to demand that I play "Welcome to the Jungle" on the stereo but he got the name wrong and would say, "Daddy, I want Malcolm to the Jungle," or simply, "I want a drum song," and then he would do his signature dance—a move that involved one foot (typically the left one) planted to the floor, as if it was nailed there, while he kicked the other leg in the air and spun around in a circle, banging his head up and down like a deranged circus animal. The music had to be fast, hard and loud. If it wasn't he would wrinkle his brow, stare hard at me and demand that I remedy the situation. "Drum Song!" he'd bark and stomp his feet until the noise gushed out from the speakers and moved him.

4. Bruce Springsteen: "Born in the U.S.A."

Perhaps it's the contradiction that hurts most, the brutal lack of irony in musical taste. Who wants to accept that the music they love often contradicts their most cherished values. Interrogators use protest music by Springsteen or bands like Rage Against the Machine to torture people who may be nothing more than protestors themselves, people who dared to speak out against the U.S. Government. You wonder if they even know how to listen, how to pay attention to the small things. Words. Tone. Rhythm. Perhaps they're just tuned into a different frequency. If you stop and think. If you stop and listen. Really listen. You hear the contradictions. You hear Springsteen singing a pop song about the pain of loss, the horror of Viet Nam, the futility of war, and the disaffection and suffering of returning soldiers. You hear the protest, the angst in the cry, "Born in the USA!" But if you don't stop, trim away all the noise, and pay attention, you don't hear the hum of morality. If you only hear the chorus, the looping sing-a-long part that has made this song one of the most popular rock songs of all time, then you're like Reagan in 1984 who famously misinterpreted and misappropriated the song when, at the height of the song's popularity, added the following lines to his standard campaign stump speech: "America's future rests in a thousand dreams inside your hearts; it rests in the message of hope in songs so many young Americans admire: New Jersey's own Bruce Springsteen. And helping you make those dreams come true is what this job of mine is all about."

5. Barney and Friends: "I love You" and Drowning Pool: "Bodies"

"In training, they forced me to listen to the Barney "I Love You" song for 45 minutes. I never want to go through that again," said one US operative.

Suzanne Cusick, a music professor at New York University, has interviewed a number of former detainees about their experiences.

Played at a certain volume, Cusick said, the music "simply prevents people from thinking."[3]

Stevie Benton's band Drowning Pool, recorded one of the interrogators' favorites, "Bodies." He had this to say about the controversy over rock songs being used to torture detainees:

"People assume we should be offended that somebody in the military thinks our song is annoying enough that played over and over it can psychologically break someone down. I take it as an honor to think that perhaps our song could be used to quell another 9/11 attack or something like that."[4]

> I take it as an honor to think
> Perhaps our song could be used to quell another attack
> I take it as an honor to think

Other artists think differently:

"The fact that music I helped create was used in crimes against humanity sickens me. We need to end torture and close Guantanamo now."
-- Tom Morello, guitarist, Rage Against the Machine

In October of 2009, Morello and a coalition of other musicians—including Trent Reznor and members of Pearl Jam, R.E.M, and The Roots—demanded that the U.S. Government release the titles of all songs used to torture detainees at the Guantanamo Bay detention facility.

---

3 http://www.chicagotribune.com/news/chi-talk-musical-tortureoct23,0,4546424.story

4 from blog at http://qwidget.com/blog/2008/12/pop-music-used-to-torture-detainees/.

6. Aerosmith, Britney Spears, Christina Aguilera, Don McLean, Lil' Kim, Limp Bizkit, Meat Loaf, Rage Against the Machine, Red Hot Chili Peppers, Nine Inch Nails, and Tupac Shakur.

These artists are also on the suspected list of most used by the U.S. military to interrogate and psychologically break down detainees in places like Abu Ghraib, Guantanamo Bay, and other detention facilities. But many of them are also on my most-used, most-listened-to list. They're classics, looped over and over on local radio stations. They're the soundtrack to school drop-offs and pick-ups, family outings, and late night drives. These songs are songs that make me smile and dance or cheer. They're songs that, at times, bring me some small amount of peace in a crazy world. But I cannot deny that many of my favorites are the favorite weapons of torturers. And I'm just beginning to understand what this means.

Perhaps the sad and terrifying truth is that my appreciation for music--this music, my music, American music—reveals that what I have in common with those interrogators is more than musical taste, more than a shared love, but also a latent propensity for violence and self-destruction. Did the music help them hurt? Did it inspire the violence? Is this an American sickness? And could I do the same if the soundtrack and scene repeated? It's always the other kids who do things like this. Other kids hurt people. Not me. I don't believe in that. I just like the music.

I know this now: the nostalgic first-time-I-heard-it memory, the image of place and person, is scrubbed over, peeled away by the sounds of torture. Those songs can never mean the same again. Not to the victims—not now that they have been played this way. And not to perpetrators. And perhaps these songs will never mean the same to any of us again either. There is no cocoon of nostalgia insulated enough to protect us from these truths. "Enter Sandman" just sounds different to me now. It just sounds wrong. Other songs, too. Perhaps the echoes from those acts resonate through all of us, coloring our own memories, tracing a jagged line between my love for Metallica, your love for another song or artist on the list, to that detainee strung up in his cell, banging his head because metal health is driving him mad. Perhaps one drop in a distant pool can discolor the vast sea of memory and we are all responsible for the alienation of nostalgia, for the separation between what we remember, what we love, and what it means anew.

STEVEN CHURCH is the author of *The Guinness Book of Me: a Memoir of Record, Theoretical Killings: Essays and Accidents, The Day After The Day After: My Atomic Angst, Ultrasonic: Essays and One with the Tiger: Sublime and Violent Encounters between Humans and Animals*. His essays have been published in *Passages North, DIAGRAM, Brevity, River Teeth, The Rumpus, AGNI, The Pedestrian, Colorado Review, Creative Nonfiction, Terrain*.org, and many others. He is a Founding Editor and Nonfiction Editor for the nationally recognized literary magazine, *The Normal School*; and he teaches for the residential MFA Program at Fresno State and for low-residency MFA Programs at Sierra Nevada College.

LEA CARPENTER

Christmas

The morning my father died I woke up before dawn. My newborn son was screaming. He was hungry. Had he not been hungry and had he not screamed and had I not woken up to feed him I would have not been in the room when my father turned towards the window (apparently this is a very common thing) and took his last breath. I had fed my little boy then gone to check on my father, he was just down the hall, I was home and sleeping in the bedroom I had slept in as a child. In the twenty-four hours preceding that hour my siblings had all come home, too. My Virginian godmother, always aware of rule and requirement, arrived and immediately ordered food for days, comfort foods like tea sandwiches and shepherds pies, platters of shrimp with pints of cocktail sauce, fried oysters and alcohol including champagne even as this was not a celebration. Everyone was spilling out of rooms, my nephew made a bed on a treadmill. And everyone knew what was happening. There is terror in the hours around a death but there is also a kind of peace. When someone slaps you in the face you take a minute to catch your breath.

The day before my mother had called and said, "it's time." It was almost Christmas and people were busy, the absolute cliché and yet absolute acceptability of too many parties causing stress. Who doesn't love Christmas, who doesn't love joy and twinkly lights. A few nights before I'd been at a dinner downtown in Manhattan where everyone talked about the now, what they wanted and expected, wants and expectations being the currency when you're young. I had stepped out of the dinner to call home. By then, it was taking him almost an hour to get down the two small flights of stairs from the bedroom to the kitchen and my mother was preparing meals at seven and eating at ten. At Thanksgiving she'd explored the cost of installing an elevator. When my father said he would never use one she told me, "he's putting us on notice."

The night before the morning my baby woke me up I'd sat on my father's bed. He was on oxygen. He wasn't talking much. Or eating, despite my mother pouring Ensure into a martini glass. When things get chaotic, we fall back on ritual. The martini was a ritual, always with three olives, always on the rocks, always Beefeater's. We knew he couldn't drink but the idea that he knew the drink was there gave us something, maybe hope. That glass was the belief that this thing wasn't moving in one direction. I gave my son my father's name.

There were four or five doctors around the house, some involved in Daddy's care and others who were friends, a Harvard psychiatrist who seemed positioned mainly to mind me, to catch my pieces if they fell apart or disappeared. I remember him standing behind me as I tried, and failed, to boil a pot of water. As the house filled with people coming by for last visits, I felt relief when my father finally told us he didn't want to see anyone anymore.

I remember my baby crying around five AM. I remember walking down the hall in my nightgown. I remember my mother in the room with my father and my sister, who is a minister. "This is it," she said, and I wanted to say, "This is what?" We held hands and then he turned toward the window. And then he was gone.

Later, before we had moved him, one of the doctors gave me a pair of scissors. She told me to cut a piece off the bathrobe he was wearing. It was navy cashmere. My mother had dressed him in it worried he was cold. It made me think of the Terracotta Army, buried alongside the First Emperor of China, there to protect him. My father had lived and worked in China. "So far I believe I am going to like my new job tremendously," he wrote home to his mother then, "all of it is outdoors, and not unlike my Western experiences. Couldn't help remembering the days when my idea of a perfect life was to ride through the hills packing a .45 and carrying a carbine, and now I'm paid to do it." What he really wanted was to be a cowboy.

"You'll want it someday," was the doctor's rationale about the bathrobe and, like a child in a cult who feels nothing and follows orders I cut along the edge of one sleeve to make a rectangle, rolled it up, and placed it in my pocket. A few phone calls were made and the first friends to come had been out shooting ducks and were still in their hunting gear and orange ball caps. They sat on the edge of that bed and wept, grown men, giants in their fields, totally broken. In those moments everyone peels back the masks. There is only emotion. If we tried to live life at that pitch all the time we'd explode.

It was raining. It was almost noon. I was still in my nightgown. We would place my father's body in a coffin and the coffin in a Hearse. My mother draped a flag over him. Everyone went out in the rain and walked alongside the car as it moved down the driveway lined by the tall oaks my father loved, the rhododendron he'd seen bloom for over fifty years. The house *was* him. When the driver flipped his blinker to turn I didn't handle that well, I didn't want that car to take him away, I wanted him back in that bed. I wanted to roll everything back. To a week before, when I didn't come home because I'd gone to that dinner party downtown. Or a month before, when I'd stayed at the beach with friends. No, to a year before when, instead of hearing an opera at the Met he loved I'd chosen to stay home and watch news. Every single choice I'd ever made suddenly seemed insane. And then, soaking wet in my nightgown, I remembered my baby, who needed to be fed. He was six months old.

My mother asked everyone into the one room my father loved, a library where he had a desk and where I once did homework alongside him after dinner. My mother asked everyone to say what they were feeling, a sort of Quaker meeting for lapsed WASPs and Catholics. I didn't know what to say so I said something he had taught me, Juliet's lines about *and, when he shall die take him and cut him into little stars*— That afternoon I wrote his obituary.

That night someone quoted Luke 2:14, it was almost Christmas Eve, after all:

> And suddenly there appeared with the angel a great multitude of the heavenly host, praising God and saying, "Glory to God in the highest, and on earth peace to men on whom His favor rests!" When the angels had left them and gone into Heaven, the shepherds said to one another, "Let us go to Bethlehem and see this thing that has happened, which the Lord has made known to us."

My father claimed he didn't believe in God. He preferred Shakespeare. But he loved the story of Christmas, and the idea of angels. He loved the simplicity of the manger as a crèche for the son of God and he loved the Wise Men with their gifts wandering the desert on camel back, the Immaculate Conception of Mary which he knew nearly everyone thought was the Immaculate Conception of Jesus. He loved the idea of shepherds minding flocks who wanted to "see this thing that has happened," a bit of Biblical understatement, or wit. My father had once experienced war but seemed to prefer peace, or maybe that was my experience of him. A desire for peace is maybe why he turned toward that window.

———————

LEA CARPENTER is the author of the novel *Eleven Days* (Vintage). Her second novel, *Red White Blue*, is forthcoming from Knopf.

MAURICE DECAUL

Traction

A play in one act

Character: Lewis 32. An analyst for a NGO

Notes: The play should not last more than one hour and fifteen minutes. The apartment should be rich with sound, although Lewis does not speak. The apartment should be new with modern fixtures, minimalist in its aesthetic.

It is late afternoon when Lewis returns home with groceries. He hangs his coat and places his boots on a towel. He retrieves a wet mop from the closet and buffs the floor where he had walked with his boots, gingerly removing the cleaning pad from it. He walks to the trash and places it in then washes his hands.

He shakes a bothersome thought out of his head.

He walks to the kitchen with his groceries and begins to unpack the bags: a pound of Arctic Char, and two lemons. One half dozen eggs and cream cheese. Four everything bagels and a package of heirloom tomatoes. He reaches into one of the bags and removes a few potatoes and a container of pulp free orange juice. He moves a bowl of butter, a head of romaine and two pounds of cherries to the counter. He unpacks a gallon of water and a pint of half and half. He opens the refrigerator and places everything within except for the Arctic Char and the lemons; he puts the everything bagels into the bread box near the toaster.

He takes a Tupperware container from the cupboard and places the Arctic Char in it. The plastic grocery bags and the butcher paper in which the Arctic Char was wrapped are placed in the trash. He washes his hands.

Lewis opens the refrigerator and takes out a piece of ginger. He smashes it on his cutting board with his chef's knife. He has another memory of the taxi exploding towards him but he shakes the memory from his head and continues chopping the ginger.

He mixes the ginger with soy sauce and red pepper flakes then massages the marinade into the flesh of the fish.

He washes the cutting board and chef's knife, dries them and then cuts a lemon into wedges. He eats two of the wedges. He opens the refrigerator and removes the bottled water, opens it and squeezes lemon juice in. The roughness of the bottle's handle reminds him of the pistol grip of his M16. He lets the thought go and places the water in the freezer. He cleans up the counter then washes his hands.

Lewis walks from his kitchen to his living room. His apartment is newly built. It's neither trendy nor extravagant but it reflects Lewis's relative affluence. Its floors are covered in grey limed oak; its ceiling is unpainted concrete. An expensive black leather sofa provides seating while a midcentury-inspired dining table set provides more.

Lewis stands in the center of the room with the television remote in hand, flipping from channel to channel before settling on cable news. The anchor reports typically damning news: another massacre, quarreling politicians, fraud, waste and abuse. Lewis, who considers himself conscientious and progressive, shakes his head.

His cellphone buzzes and he takes it from his jeans and responds to the text message. He turns the ringer up and walks to the kitchen and plugs the phone into a wall socket.

He takes a mug from the cupboard and fills it with water then places the cup and water in the microwave. He sets the microwave for two minutes and pushes the start button.

He takes the Tupperware container out of the refrigerator, opens it and smells the Arctic Char before placing it back in the refrigerator. He removes the half and half and opens it.

The microwave beeps and Lewis takes the hot water to the counter and spoons in two table spoons of coffee and two table spoons of sugar in the raw. He stirs in a splash of half and half.

His cell phone chirps and he answers the text message. He takes a sip of coffee and walks to the center of the living room.

He stands with the remote in hand and switches the channel to sports. After a minute he switches back to cable news.

His cell phone chirps so he walks to the kitchen to answer the text message.

Realizing that he had forgotten to place the half and half in the refrigerator he does so and takes a handful of cherries. He eats the cherries and drinks the coffee in the kitchen while still watching cable news. He finishes his cherries and his coffee placing the pits in the trash.

He washes his hands.

He places the cup and spoon in the dishwasher then washes his hands again.

He looks over his shoulder at something said by a pundit on the cable news channel and sees the taxi exploding towards him. He closes his eyes and then opens them.

He takes a breath.

Lewis turns on the oven and sets the temperature. He takes the Tupperware with the Arctic Char from the fridge. He opens the Tupperware and smells the Arctic Char. He takes a Dutch oven from the cupboard and places the Arctic Char inside. He drips the remaining soy sauce and ginger on to the Arctic Char before placing the lid on the Dutch oven. He places the Tupperware in the dishwasher and washes his hands. He sets a timer on the oven and places the Dutch oven inside. He walks to the window in the living room and opens it slightly to cool the apartment.

He goes into his bedroom for several moments; he removes his clothes places his jeans and button down shirt on hangers and hangs the hangers in his closet. His undershirt, socks and underwear get balled up and placed in the hamper. He wraps his towel around his torso and exits his bedroom, but on his way to the bathroom, he stops in front of the television to watch cable news. Lewis shakes his head in disbelief as the news reports another mass killing; a blast of very cold air forces a shiver so he crosses the living room to close the open window. The oven beeps indicating it has completed cooking the aArctic Char. Lewis shakes the cold off of his body. The cell phone beeps and Lewis walks to the kitchen to answer the message.

He walks into the bathroom to shower and locks the door. The toilet flushes and we overhear Lewis washing his hands. While Lewis is in the shower his cell phone beeps then it rings.

Lewis is followed out of the bathroom by a cloud of steam. The apartment is cold from earlier and he shivers. He walks to the thermostat and turns the temperature up five degrees.

The smell of the Arctic Char is compelling enough for Lewis to want to remove it from the oven to taste. He salts it and returns it to the oven. He takes the lemon water from the freezer and places it in the refrigerator.

A group of people are in the hallway outside of Lewis's apartment. Their conversation is indistinct, but their voices are recognizable as female. Lewis walks to the front door and looks through the peephole. He touches himself. His cellphone beeps and Lewis is surprised by the many messages and missed calls. He answers the text then unplugs the phone from the wall socket and heads to his bedroom to dress.

He dresses in sweats and t-shirt and walks out of his bedroom with his phone in hand texting back and forth. He takes a seat on the couch and closes the phone and switches the channel on the television from cable news to sports. His phone beeps and he returns the text. He flips the channel on the television from sports to cable news then gets up and walks to the dining area and sets the table for two. At this moment, he realizes that he has been thinking about the taxi exploding towards him again; he stands still for a moment and lets out a breath.

Lewis walks to the thermostat and turns the temperature down five degrees then opens the window to vent the heat.

Lewis begins to cut the potatoes into wedges. He seasons the potatoes with salt, pepper, rosemary and olive oil and pours the wedges into stoneware. He places the stoneware into the toaster oven and sets the temperature and timer. He preps the salad and raspberry vinaigrette. He washes his hands. His phone beeps and he answers the text, the taxi explodes towards him.

Lewis walks to the thermostat and turns the temperature up five degrees then closes the window. He turns down the lights in the apartment then sits on the couch and flips the television from cable news to sports. He gets up and walks to his desk and picks up a book. He switches the television off and begins to read. He feels the dull pain of a migraine reveal itself behind his left eye. He clutches at his eye and groans. He closes the book and takes a bottle of over-the-counter pain reliever from his work bag. He opens the bottle and spills four pills into the palm of his hand. He downs the pills with a cup of water and lays down on the couch. He gets up and takes his Ray Bans from his work bag and puts them on. He switches off the light and sits in the dark.

The toaster oven rings. Lewis bolts up and dashes to the bathroom to vomit. He wretches several times into the toilet. He flushes the toilet. He brushes his teeth and washes his hands. He stumbles from the bathroom to the kitchen and makes himself a cup of coffee. He walks back to the couch sipping the coffee. His phone beeps. He reads the text then tosses his phone against the wall. He rubs his eyes and forehead.

Lewis walks in to the bedroom and comes out wearing a sweater. He spills four more pain pills into his hand and downs them with the rest of his coffee. He picks up his car keys and puts on his heavy winter coat. He slips his feet into his boots and not caring so much about the mess he is making, walks to the living room and retrieves his broken phone. He places it in his pocket and walks out the door.

Hours later, Lewis lets himself into the apartment. He removes his boots and heavy winter coat. He steps carefully trying to not step with his sock feet in the puddle. He goes into the bathroom and washes his hands. He places the roasted potatoes and Arctic Char into the refrigerator. He drinks a cup of orange juice. He massages his temples and eyes. He is lost in thoughts about the increasing severity of his migraines. He is beginning to believe he might need to see a neurologist to make sure he does not have a brain tumor. He opens his eyes and sees the exploding taxi.

MAURICE DECAUL, a former Marine, is a poet, essayist, and playwright, whose writing has been featured in the *New York Times*, *The Daily Beast*, *Sierra Magazine*, *Epiphany*, *Callaloo*, *Narrative* and others. His poems have been translated into French and Arabic and his theatrical works, *Holding it Down* and *Sleep Song*, collaborations with composer Vijay Iyer and poet Mike Ladd, have been produced and performed at New York City's Harlem Stage, Washington DC's ATLAS INTERSECTIONS FESTIVAL, in Paris and in Antwerp. His play *Dijla Wal Furat, Between the Tigris and the Euphrates* was produced in New York City by Poetic Theater Productions in the winter of 2015. Maurice is a graduate of Columbia University and New York University, and is currently studying at Brown University.

RACHAEL HANEL

In the Balance

In 2007, two professors in the Midwest published a study where they asked college students questions about a scientific theory known as the balance of nature. This theory states that nature is always correcting itself: ecosystems may swing wildly, but like two kids on a teeter-totter, everything hinges on a fulcrum. Animal populations, plant biomass, temperatures—up and down, up and down, up and down.

In the study's introduction, the professors—one in psychology, one in ecology—contended the balance of nature theory is a metaphor, a cultural myth that stretches back thousands of years and one that still guides students' perceptions today. One of the ecology professors noticed her students clinging to this theory, even though in class she said that scientists have largely discredited the claims behind it. She wanted to know how students defined balance of nature and whether they believed the theory was a legitimate scientific thought.

When asked for their definitions of balance of nature, students responded with phrases such as "needs of a being are satisfied," and where everything lives "properly" and in "harmony." Balance of nature is a state, they said, "where each species is thriving" and "no one species is dominating," resulting in equal birth and death rates. In this state, "the 'circle of life' would be constant" and order prevails. One student defined balance of nature as the "absence of environmental and human disturbances." The ecology professor thought this last answer was especially strange, given that in class she emphasized the fact that weather and climate constantly disrupt animal and plant systems. This disconnect puzzled her. She needed to find out what was going on in her students' minds.

* * *

War'n'peace. The words blend into one without effort. The syllables roll off our tongues with equal weight, neither one dominating. If we want to break them apart, we have to say them slowly and concentrate in order to articulate them precisely. They are a pair. If you have one, you'll have the other. To me, when they're spoken together like this, it suggests a balance. Again, I see two kids on a teeter-totter—one goes up, one goes down, taking turns at the fulcrum's tipping point.

But maybe they are opposites, which is different than a balance. Two things that are opposites never come together. They will forever remain apart, no fulcrum in sight.

* * *

Like the kids on the teeter-totter, the world constantly moves. If balance is achieved, it's only for the briefest moment of time. Those kids don't just sit on the teeter-totter and get stuck achieving stasis. The bigger, stronger kid has the advantage.

If there were true balance in nature, species would never die off. Diseases, storms, and climate change all disrupt ecosystems. But even without those disturbances, another theory says that plants and animals always live in a state of fluctuation and cannot achieve balance even if left alone. This theory, only a few decades old, was given the ominous-sounding name of chaos theory. When scientists further studied and tested this theory, the level of chaos present in nature shocked them.

In one study conducted in the early 1990s, scientists at the University of Minnesota planted ten plots of the same prairie grass, only changing the amount of nitrogen in the soil. The low-nitrogen soil produced a fairly stable grass population over the five years of the study. However, grass in the soil with the richest, healthiest nitrogen saw massive swings of biomass, nearly disappearing completely at one point.

"I never imagined I would find chaos," one of the scientists said. "I imagined it would grow up to equilibrium. This has changed my world view, to be blunt about it."

* * *

The evidence on war and peace is clear: chaos rules. According to author Chris Hedges, the world has been at peace for only eight percent of recorded history—268 years out of the past 3,400.

But like those Midwestern students in the balance of nature study, we want to believe in metaphor and myth. We let the metaphors and myths and aphorisms guide us. They bring order to a world dominated by chaos. Chaos breeds questions and as humans, we want answer, or at the very least, hope.

Like those students, I cling to the idea of balance, that there's still a chance things will even out. Maybe in the next 3,400 years, we'll have war only eight percent of the time. I want to believe war will attract peace.

* * *

Time and again I return to Kahlil Gibran's meditation on joy and sorrow:
"When you are joyous, look deep in your heart and you shall find it is only that which has given you sorrow that is giving you joy. When you are sorrowful look ahead in your heart, and you shall see that in truth you are weeping for that which has been your delight."
I first read this a few years after my dad died. I was 15 years old when he died and spent the next few years navigating the waves of that ripping loss. I grew up in a stoic Minnesota household and was not accustomed to deep emotions of sadness and grief. Or love, for that matter. But Gibran's words made me realize my depths of sorrow were born out of the love I had for Dad. My grief is painful, but having had that time with Dad is worth the pain.
I used to think that Gibran was saying joy and sorrow achieve balance. That you have equal amounts of the two in your life. But I don't think that's true anymore. I know people plagued by one calamity after another. Sorrow seems to dominate; it's the stronger kid on the teeter-totter. It's hard to admit that in the 27 years since Dad died that I've felt more grief than I have felt joy, but it's true.

* * *

The authors of the balance of nature study didn't venture any conclusions as to why the students believed in the theory despite evidence to the contrary. In the study's conclusion, the authors pointed out that students did not see balance of nature as a mere metaphor— it was a way they described real ecological systems. However, they all did not arrive at a common definition.
The study's authors did not drill down deeper as to *why* students believed the way that they did. I can venture some guesses. Like the students, I live in the Midwest. The heartland straddles the 45th parallel, which is equidistant from the equator and the North Pole, and it's deep inland. As a result, the four seasons are almost perfectly balanced. You can count on winter, spring, summer, fall—always. Of course there are variations

in temperature, rain, and snow from year to year, but there's also a lot of consistency. Corn and soybeans get planted, they grow, and they are harvested. It will snow and turn cold, so you can ski every year. The snow will melt, so you can get out on your bike and ride as far as you want on that first glorious spring day. The lakes will warm, and you'll put on your swimsuit and find respite from stifling summer heat. In the fall, you move the sweaters to the front of the closet and gather gloves and jackets. Warmth and cold, planting and harvest, sun rising and setting. In the Midwest, it's easy to subscribe to this form of magical thinking.

Too, a balance of nature represents hope. Maybe these students are just hopeful, and I see the beauty in it. In class, their professor provided evidence that proved the balance of nature theory false. Still, they shunned chaos, chose not to believe that animal and plant species will die off. Or, maybe they can see that it has happened but believe nature will somehow manage to correct itself and restore order. Just as I hope and want to believe that my sorrow is equal to my joy, as I hope and want to believe that peace will, eventually, rise to the top. So I do.

––––––––––

RACHAEL HANEL lives and writes just outside of Mankato, Minnesota. She is a former newspaper reporter and copy editor and teaches Mass Media at Minnesota State University, Mankato. She is the author of more than 20 nonfiction books for children. *We'll Be the Last Ones to Let You Down: Memoir of a Gravedigger's Daughter* (University of Minnesota Press), is her first book for adults. Rachael holds a bachelor's degree in mass communications and history and a master's degree in history, both from Minnesota State University, Mankato. She earned a Ph.D. in Creative Writing from Bath Spa University.

www.ingramcontent.com/pod-product-compliance
Lightning Source LLC
Chambersburg PA
CBHW050039040726
47599CB00015B/1744